PRAISE FOR FIONA CARR AND *THE MAD MARQUIS*!

"This book has snappy dialogue and a wonderful cast of un-stereotypical characters. It's fast-paced, a compelling page-turner, and just plain fun!"

—*Romantic Times*

"In the capable hands of Fiona Carr, readers receive a terrific tale starring a strong cast that leads to a delightful novel . . . a fabulous nineteenth-century romance."

—*Midwest Book Review*

"*The Mad Marquis* is an enjoyable historical romance . . . a sparkling romantic gem."

—*ARomanceReview.com*

Other *Leisure* books by Fiona Carr:

THE MAD MARQUIS

STOLEN KISSES

Hinges creaked, and the hasp locked, and Sophie was trapped inside the kissing gate by the most devastatingly handsome man she had ever known.

Up close, Lionel's face had the same arrogant blade of a nose that she remembered, but age had more sharply chiseled the angles of his cheeks and jaw. A new scar split one brow. From that almost fatal incident in the war, she thought with a chill. His well-shaped mouth turned down with a cynicism Sophie had never seen.

"You were to wait for me," he said, his gray eyes hard.

His reproof rubbed her wrong. She had waited once. "You were very late."

"Which doesn't change the fact that I invited you to my home, and you saw fit to leave. Not a promising start to our new alliance."

"I agreed to no alliance, my lord."

His face flushed. His eyes narrowed. "Then you will not agree to this."

Before she could suck in a breath of surprise, he lowered his head and sought her mouth. His lips were knowing, questing, and he pressed his tall frame to her breasts, radiating heat into her body. He deepened his kiss, his claim, and her head spun in amazement.

THE KISSING GATE

FIONA CARR

LEISURE BOOKS · NEW YORK CITY

With thanks to Virginia Kantra,
Wendy Lindstrom, Nancy Northcott,
and Susan Sipal for making a fun book more fun.

A LEISURE BOOK®

April 2004

Published by

Dorchester Publishing Co., Inc.
200 Madison Avenue
New York, NY 10016

ISBN 0-8439-5289-X

Visit us on the web at www.dorchesterpub.com.

THE
KISSING
GATE

ACKNOWLEDGMENTS

*To Loraine Fletcher of Reading, England;
and Carolyn Franklin of Swansea, Wales,
for showing me real kissing gates
and sharing my enthusiasm for this story.*

Chapter One

That Bosom, which so Fair excels;
Those Breasts, than Snow more soft and white;
Whose new-born Roundness heaves and swells,
And captives Mortals with the Sight:
By those Twin-Jewels bright I thee implore,
Extinguish all my Flames, my dying Powers restore.
*   —The Pleasures of Coition (1721)*

Wraxham House, April 1816

Lionel Westfall, newly elevated earl of Wraxham, buttoned a
recently purchased shooting jacket of finest Scottish tweed. A
statement, as he forcibly returned to country life, that he still
had his standards.

It was blasted untimely for his father to turn up his toes on
the heels of his wife's unseemly departure.

And damned annoying now that he was earl that everyone
wanted something from him. Including his brother-in-law.

1

"I'm not cut out to stand as magistrate, Harry. Besides, I look hagged in black."

Henry Pelham, marquis of Rayne, smiled faintly at Lionel's cynical city slang. "The lord lieutenant of the county highly recommends you for the task."

Lionel snapped open his enameled snuffbox. "You are the lord lieutenant of the county."

"Precisely. And as long as Squire Upton can't sit on that buckshot bum of his, I want a man in his position who can look upon our little local problems with fresh eyes."

"Little local problems indeed. Weights and measures, petty theft, village quarrels and grievances. Surely knowledge of the neighborhood is a better recommendation."

"Did I mention poaching, burglaries, the odd abduction?"

Lionel squelched a momentary interest. "I've been widowed only a month—"

"And earl for a mere twenty-two days. I can see how cut up you are about your losses."

Lionel couldn't meet his old friend's ironic gaze. He *was* cut up. His wife's and father's deaths had turned his life upside down. He was swapping twenty years of urban entertainments for rural monotony, extravagant estate debts to meet, and six sons to care for.

Or rather, six strangers to shepherd into manhood.

"Penelope's death was a shock," Lionel said solemnly.

"Your father's wasn't."

"No, the old chap had been dying for years."

Harry slapped a leather glove into his palm. "As you have, my man."

His words caught Lionel up short. He wasn't immune to home truths, but he'd honed his dark wit in London's most exclusive gentlemen's clubs.

"Not dead, Harry. Just deadened."

Quick sympathy flared in Harry's eyes. "That bad, eh?"

Not so he'd ever talk about it. Think about it, yes. Berate and blame himself, yes. But talk it over, even with his oldest friend, never. Penelope had gone to her grave without his saying a word against the mother of his sons, and there she would lie, nothing but her actions to condemn her.

Lionel turned to the wall of windows in his library and looked out over Wraxham's grounds. Gentle green downs stretched before him, a dozen furlongs from the sea. They were his realm now, his responsibility.

As were his sons, at last.

Harry came and stood beside him.

"This is my chance to start over, Harry, with myself, with them," Lionel said, giving quiet, determined voice to his new plan, his old dream of a family united, in harmony.

"The magistracy would be a fresh start too."

Lionel snapped his neglected snuffbox closed. "What do I know of country folk and county matters?"

"It's not what you know. It's what they need. As magistrate you could give them an example of duty and responsibility. It is a temporary post."

"You would do as well as I. Better, for you never left the county."

"Not a chance. Julia's due in a few short weeks—or long ones as the event may prove." Harry swelled with pride. "Our first was early, our second late. Early or late, I'll be there."

"I promised to take time to get to know my boys."

"I thought the three eldest were at school."

For now. "Yes, three hellions there, and two hellions at home."

"That's only five. I take it one of your sons doesn't follow in your footsteps."

Harry was one of the few people on earth who knew where Lionel's steps had trod, Harry and his three younger brothers. Boyhood neighbors and compatriots, they'd been hellions together.

But they hadn't been spoiled like his sons. They hadn't been brats. "The youngest misses his mother. Simon is seven, and troubled."

3

And his eleven-year-old twins, still at home, were unpredictable. At least Graeme, his eighteen-year-old heir, was off at the university. His next two, Marcus and James, fifteen and fourteen when they'd come home for winter holiday, were safely ensconced at Abercairn, longtime school for Wraxham's sons near their Scottish properties.

"Ah." Harry walked away, hands clasped behind his back. "It's mostly papers you can read at home at night. That, and the Wednesday afternoon courts twice a month. Plenty of time for the boys after their tutor's done with them."

Which raised the latest sore spot, actually a gnawing aggravation. "Their latest tutor fled."

Harry raised a brow. "Didn't take to country living?"

Lionel snorted in disgust. "Didn't take to toads in trousers, the last in a line of tricks my jackanapes played on him."

"Ha. Our trick of slithering snakes in nightshirts topped that." Harry clapped a hand on his shoulder. "Boys will be boys, my friend. We were. And look how we turned out."

"Speaking strictly for myself, I turned out to be a cynical gambler with a taste for too-fine clothes, too-fast horses, and too-expensive women. Not what I want for my sons."

Harry didn't blink. "You just haven't found their match. There's a hardened old gent of a tutor out there waiting for them. But the county can't wait on you. Upton's been laid up a month, and the docket's piling up."

"Ballocks, Harry. This county's full of eligible men."

Harry looked at the ceiling and said quietly, "Your old man let the county down, as much as, maybe more than, he did you. He didn't set a standard, didn't rally for his neighbors, didn't back his tenants. The title is not regarded as it was."

"I know." And he regretted it. It might not have been his fault, but it had become his responsibility.

"As long as you're reforming everything else, why not take a shot at that?"

* * *

Why not take a shot at that?

Disputed deeds, disputed wills, disputed marriage settlements. A raft of human discontent, Lionel thought with faint distaste two weeks later in the great room at Squire Upton's grange.

He riffled through the mound of papers on the desk, his attention fixed on the cases that would come before him in this, his second court session as magistrate. Petitioners milled outside the great oak doors, impatient for the Wednesday session to begin, which he'd scheduled weekly until he caught up.

At his insistence, they still convened in the great hall at Squire Upton's grange. He didn't want anyone to assume that his appointment was anything but temporary.

Yet to his great surprise, he was not bored. Among other matters, reams of litigious documents were putting his unlamented wife's talents in perspective.

How had she managed to stamp her will on everyone and everything without ending up in court?

How had he managed to allow it?

Yesterday he'd marched through his fields with Harry, his old war injury crying out for easy London life. Having had six sons himself, he'd hoped to calm the father-to-be with a round of shooting on the eve of his third child's birth.

To Lionel's jaded amusement, his brother-in-law was wound like clockworks over this third blessed event. Only the most appalling blather on Lionel's part—in which he stooped to distastefully personal revelations—distracted Harry from his vigil. In fact, the subject of Lionel as widower, newly liberated from onerous leg shackles, had inspired happily married Harry to rare eloquence.

"Marriage thrives on compromise, on partnership, on a loving give and take," he had insisted.

Harry and Julia's union might do just that. But Lionel's match had soured, and he knew why. He'd taken the path of least resistance. He'd given in to his father in an attack of duty.

5

He'd given in to his wife in a fit of bloody idiocy. On his wedding night, he'd relinquished his natural right to rule the roost for her promise of hot, obliging sex. Which she'd given, and he'd got.

Incredibly, even for a randy twenty-one-year-old, hot sex with a willing wife he neither loved nor respected had proved not to be enough. He'd felt isolated in his marriage and rebuffed in his bed, a stallion serving selfish needs that had everything to do with the deal they'd made and nothing to do with loyalty, respect, or even simple affection.

Baffled by his yearning for some deeper human connection, he'd filled an empty parade of days and nights with decadent London entertainments: cards, carriages, and courtesans. Not that he wasn't good at gaming and racing and cynical sex. In his set, he'd set the style.

The style, and not the substance.

He had wasted his life. Yesterday he'd tramped home across the downs on a rare golden afternoon, with a leash of pheasant and a brace of duck, England all emerald about him. Stricken by his own emptiness in the midst of Wraxham's beauty, he'd been barely able to look his anxious, besotted brother-in-law in the face. He envied him, admired him.

He reproached himself. Harry's comfortable worn tweeds had made Lionel feel the fop in his natty new hunting jacket. Harry's devotion to his family made Lionel feel the fool.

What had he missed? How had he missed it?

Why had he allowed his wife to manage their life? Had his will failed? Had he shirked duty?

Or was he just naturally his father's son, a shortsighted, self-indulgent wastrel?

The clock in the squire's grange hall chimed two. Lionel buttoned his black robes, pocketed his snuffbox, and peeled off his reading glasses. Not that style counted here. Not here in the country, far from London and the ton.

Substance was what he sought, what he hoped to offer. Fairness, insight, perhaps even wisdom—he could dredge those up without disturbing his deadened heart.

The bailiff swung open carved oak doors, darkened by centuries of smoke in the old grange.

The milling crowd shuffled into line. After everyone who could fit had crowded in, the line snaked into the hallway out of sight, an endless chain of human discord and discontent. To Lionel's amazement, he could fix some of their problems. Farmer Blevins's ram kept breaking out of its pen and trying to woo every ewe from Wraxham to the sea in or out of season. With dispatch, Lionel instructed the man to build the randy fellow a sturdier enclosure or forfeit it the next time it got out.

Meanwhile, fire had destroyed the farrier's forge, and Owen Hill, the beefy butcher, was breathing down his neck to collect a debt. Lionel exhorted Hill to grant the man some leniency, which he agreed to do. Briefly Lionel savored an altruistic sense of power. He was starting to find for the plaintiff who had bought a landlocked property unawares when all eyes turned to see the commotion beyond the great oak doors.

It was a woman's voice, he could tell that much. Neither young nor old, but anger marked its educated accents. Then a boy's voice protested.

A familiar boy's voice. Lionel's blood chilled.

Maxim's voice, or Alexander's. His twins. Eleven-year-old rapscallions, sturdy towheads, their clothing always smudged or torn, shoes scuffed, excuses ready.

They'd been caught again, doing Lord knew what, and put up for public view.

He ground his teeth in disgust. This was what came of the parade of dandified, exclusive tutors that he'd let Penelope hire and fire in droves. Except that last one, whom he'd hired himself, and who had fled within a week of country toads and torments.

The crowd buzzed with curiosity, and petitioners' heads craned back to see. A dull dread threaded through him.

For an instant, he wondered what Penelope would have

done. Bugger that, he thought, checking himself. She would have gotten them off. She always had. Which explained a lot about what her sons were doing here this afternoon. Their little lives and large expectations were about to change.

He was father and magistrate, and his little hellions had taken their last free ride.

The crowd parted to make way for the angry woman and her hostages. He couldn't see her face beneath the concealing brim of her chip straw bonnet. He thought he detected wisps of nut-brown hair, dislodged no doubt by his sons' resistance, and he could tell she had started out her day neatly. But she was not richly dressed. Judging from the crowd's deference, he guessed she was a villager, probably a gentlewoman of some intermediate standing.

He fumed to think what his sons had done to her.

He fixed on his culprits. Max was usually the ringleader. Her arm clasped him around his waist, and the little miscreant was actually kicking into her skirts. An image of pale womanly legs purpled with rude bruises appalled him.

No dessert for a month, for lunch or tea or dinner.

Alex she dragged by his collar. He was arguing, and Lionel strained to hear the words, words he strongly suspected warranted mouthfuls of soap.

The trio approached, a few contended steps forward and a few disputed steps back. He gawked at her womanly torso twisting in its filmy dress.

Then he made out the face beneath the hat's crisp brim.

Sophie Bowerbank, a woman grown, coral lips parting in accusation, honey-brown eyes dark with disapproval.

His heart leaped to his throat like a schoolboy's.

"Squire Up—" She broke off, as stunned as he. "Li—Lionel, I mean, my lord."

Then she executed the briefest graceful curtsey he had ever seen in a woman encumbered with two pairs of flailing arms and kicking feet.

8

"Miss Bowerbank," he said roughly, inordinately pleased that she had recognized him on the spot.

Max looked up, his shock worth a winning hand at cards. "Father," he gulped.

"F-father!" Alex sputtered.

"Fa . . . ther? These are yours?" Sophie Bowerbank exclaimed. "I might have guessed."

Petitioners' whispers buffeted about the vaulted hall. *Wraxham's twins . . . Running wild . . . What else did we expect?*

So much for restoring respect to his father's name.

Drawing on manners refined in the most harrowing salons in London, he addressed Sophie gently. "I wish I could say this is a pleasure."

Her face flushed bright red. "It's no tea party for me."

"So I see." He crooked a finger at the bailiff to apprehend the boys. "Perhaps you could explain the . . . offense."

"The crime, my lord." Her bosom still heaved with the effort of restraining her captives. "Boys!" she snapped before the bailiff could intervene. "Silence for the magistrate."

The boys, the bailiff, and the crowd went deathly still. From the dais he glared down at his twins. "Explain yourselves."

Max, the elder by eighteen minutes, plunged in. "We were throwing rocks, sir."

The lad had gumption, he'd give him that.

Sophie's chip straw bonnet sat askew, and tendrils of plain brown hair stuck to her face. But she drew herself up. All of herself, Lionel couldn't help noticing. She'd added a stone or two to the wispy girl's physique that he remembered, and added it to advantage. She was taller, rounder, and her breasts . . . gads, those breasts . . .

In the future in his court, he would require neckerchiefs, no, shawls, no, spencers buttoned to their wearers' throats, topped by winter mufflers.

"They were using the Misses Gatewoods' freshly washed laundry for—"

He held up one hand, palm out. "Thank you, Miss Bower-bank. If my boys did something out of—"

Sophie broke in fearlessly. "*If,* my lord?"

"—*line,*" he said with emphasis, "I expect them to explain themselves. Alexander?"

Alex looked from his captor to his judge, clearly trying to gauge the heat of the frying pan relative to the fire. "Sheets make very fine targets, sir, and they wash quite clean."

Lionel struggled to pay attention to the boy as Sophie pushed him forward. But her breasts trembled practically within reach of Lionel's fingertips. Twenty years, and he hadn't forgotten that summer he'd met her at the kissing gate. What fine breasts she'd had, pale globes, plump as summer fruit and tipped with a sweet coral that matched her lips. Of course, she had been much too young. But the whole rum business had been his initiative, his fault . . .

His fixation, on Sophie Bowerbank.

It returned full force.

"Torn sheets don't wash quite clean, young man." She was reprimanding Alex. "Someone has to mend them, if they can be saved at all. They were the only sheets those poor little old ladies had."

Petitioners throughout the grange hall muttered disapproval.

Alex studied the vaulted ceiling. Max looked at his scuffed shoes.

Lionel was impressed. Their most credentialed tutor had never evoked such shame. Even so, Sophie could be exaggerating. The old ladies could be her friends. "Are you quite sure, Miss Bowerbank, of the extent of the damage?"

"Quite sure, my lord, of the damage and who did it." Sophie forged furiously ahead. "If you stop round at the Misses Gate-woods', next door to the rectory, you will see the proof."

Lionel paused for a very long time, far more aware of the indignant rise and fall of her bosom than a magistrate ought to be.

10

Not one to be intimidated, she assessed him back, and waited for his answer.

"I will take your word on this, Miss Bowerbank. My boys are . . . adventurous."

"*Adventurous*, my lord?" she shot back, her creamy skin flushing with indignation. "Just what I would have expected of a father in your position. I caught those boys red-handed. Miss Gatewood and Miss Phoebe Gatewood were in tears. A fair magistrate would see that they are recompensed."

"A fair magistrate would question the accused before condemning them. Maxim, Alexander."

"Sir" and, "Sir," they said.

"Did you throw stones at any ladies' laundry in the village this afternoon?"

"Sheets, sir," said Max gamely. "We wouldn't have used those ladies' sheets, sir, if we had known."

"In future, you can assume that any and all sheets hung out to dry belong to some lady who does not want them stoned."

Alex ducked his head and murmured, "They flapped so in the breeze, Father. 'Twas quite a challenge hitting one square on."

Lionel blew out a breath in sympathy. Only yesterday he'd enjoyed the sport of bagging two pheasants himself. "Did you in fact tear the sheets?"

Squirming, Max glanced at his brother and back. "Well, sir. Yes, sir. I think it quite likely, sir."

"Do you have any notion what those sheets cost?" Lionel asked, not that he knew either. But what was a drop in the bucket to him could feed two aging spinsters for a month.

The boys shook their heads.

"You shall have to either mend the sheets with your own hands or replace them from your funds."

"But, sir . . ." they protested in unison.

"You are grounded till the Misses Gatewoods are fully recompensed."

11

Their amber eyes, so like their mother's, goggled with indignation.

Behind them, Sophie's tempting lips seemed to fight a smile of triumph. Which grated on him. It was awkward that his sons had been brought up before him on only his second week as magistrate. It was annoying that Sophie Bowerbank had, in effect, arrested and presented them.

It was appalling that she'd been right.

"And, Miss Bowerbank," he added sotto voce. The crowd rose on tiptoes, straining to hear. "If you ever catch my sons in their little peccadilloes again, kindly do not drag them on public display before their father unannounced."

"Little peccadilloes?" Sophie glowered handsomely. Her color was up, and her thick nut-brown hair tumbled down about her shoulders. "You expect more mischief in the future? Perhaps assuming, *'Cui peccare licet peccat minus.'* "

Ovid. She was spouting Ovid at him. The girl who'd conjugated Latin verbs with him by the stream had turned out a bluestocking after all.

A kernel of an idea sprouted. "No, Miss Bowerbank, I do not assume, with Ovid, that one who is allowed to sin, sins less. I do not allow my sons to sin, willy-nilly, hoping to put a stop to future crimes. But boys, even when carefully watched, will test set limits at every opportunity. What is needed is discipline and education."

"Neither of which appears to be working, my lord," she shot back, but quietly.

She was bold, and he liked it. He especially liked the way that boldness had harnessed his sons' wild energy. "Which is where you come in."

"I, my lord?"

"You seem to be an expert Latinist."

A peachy blush stained her cheek. "I know a little."

The standard, modest gentlewoman's answer. "I know better. You were your father's best student."

"He encouraged me."

"In French, Italian, geography, I presume? Perhaps with a smattering of history."

She didn't deny it. Her spinster's modesty gave way to a passionate, if whispered, pride. "Natural history, my lord. We'd rather study the florae and faunae."

He had an eyeful of fauna he itched to learn more about. "But no history?"

"I have an aversion to wars."

"Touché," he said without thinking. His father—and hers— had discovered them that summer and joined their moral, civil, and parental forces to banish him to war. She'd wept and argued, and he'd vehemently protested his father's threats and ultimatums, to no avail.

"I dislike the bloody waste myself," he added. As her learning, undirected and unused, would be a bloody waste. He fingered the top button of his unaccustomed robe, his mind made up. "Your accomplishments will do quite nicely. You are familiar with Wraxham House, I understand."

The crowd grew restless, jockeying for position to see and hear.

Sophie spoke softer, faster. "I catalogued your father's library. He had no complaints."

"Nor do I expect to." None whatsoever.

Her brows knotted—high winged brows, brows he would have found dazzlingly seductive on, say, a courtesan in town. "My lord?"

It was damned vexing to have to order his long-ago love to help, but as magistrate, as earl, as her father's employer, he had the power. "You may be my sons' new tutor."

Said sons wriggled in protest, like frogs caught in a net.

He pinned them with a monitory glare.

"But I . . . Surely not I . . ." she stammered, flummoxed by his proposal.

"Tutors with knowledge, common sense, and discipline are in short supply this year. You appear proficient in all three."

"Surely a scholar . . . a London scholar would be more . . . suitable."

"Perhaps," he said, but hiring a woman, and one so comely, gave a whole new meaning to any notion of suitability.

She scowled, perplexed. "You cannot think that I—I brought them here only on the Misses Gatewoods' account. I was just the vessel . . ."

Wrong word. Even as restless villagers pressed forward, his eyes closed on an erotic image in which Sophie became the vessel of his inconvenient mounting desire. He'd be mad to install her at Wraxham House when the merest sight of her—and in public too—sparked his carnal appetites. He imagined mad dashes into London to meet up with the ever-willing duchess of Morace. He imagined bringing his latest conquest, the actress Ariadne, here.

Ballocks, he'd sworn off decadence. There could be no going back. Meeting his sons' needs, not feeding his jaded appetites, was his concern now.

"You caught my sons and brought them here," he reminded Sophie. "That augers well for your ability to manage them."

She straightened, recovering. "I've worked with the village children only. I'm no tutor for young gentlemen."

"But you will do this for my family," he said firmly.

She set her chin. "I think not, my lord."

He straightened in surprise. Had she forgotten her place, to say nothing of his authority? *He* had forgotten both, sparring with her before these shambling ranks of villagers. He would get her consent elsewhere, he told himself, and confidently changed course.

"Very well then. We're quite done with the boys. Miss Bowerbank, would you be so kind as to escort them home?"

The miscreants groaned, as did their future tutor.

"Merely to ensure no further mishaps," he went on. "And, Maxim, tell Mrs. Plumridge to entertain our guest with tea until I can return home to thank her."

His sons must have heard his resolve. Alex leaned in and

whispered miserably, "We're too old for a woman tutor, Papa."

Lionel arched a brow. "You're too old to be caught throwing stones at ladies' sheets. I'll see you at home."

Max scuffed his toe on the worn stone floor in mute, hopeless protest.

Alex glared at a point behind Lionel's head.

Sophie kept her wits about her. Saying something he couldn't hear, she persuaded the boys to march out of the great hall with considerably more discipline than they'd marched in. But with no less attention from the crowd. Remarks followed them, and then a smattering of applause.

Lionel barely noticed. He was struggling to ignore Sophie's gently swaying hips beneath that flimsy muslin gown.

With a Herculean effort, he called his next case.

Chapter Two

So as it was one Day my pleasing Chance,
To meet a handsome young Man in a Grove,
Both time and place conspir'd to advance
The innocent Designs of charming Love.
I thought my Happiness was then compleat,
Because 'twas in his Pow'r to make it so;
I ask'd the Spark if he would do the Feat,
But the unperforming Blockhead answer'd, No.
—The Fifteen Plagues of a Maiden-Head (1707)

The twins fled into the enormous warren of Wraxham House. Sophie tapped her foot on the posh carpet of the drawing room, waiting for Lionel under his housekeeper's watchful eye. Time out of mind, Sophie had worked on the vestry committee at St. Philip's with the vinegary Mrs. Plumridge. Making small talk with the old biddy was as tedious as carding dirty wool.

Waiting was worse, but Sophie had to make a show of complying with the earl. Her father's living was wholly under Wraxham's control. As the moments ticked by on a fine ormolu clock on the mantel, she keenly felt his power over her father and herself. If only she had an excuse to leave.

At Upton Grange, she'd plainly said no to Lionel's preposterous demand.

He had presumed she meant yes. Had presumed she'd wait. Had presumed her life was at his disposal, as if she were part and parcel of her father's living.

Mrs. Plumridge was complaining that the vestry needed a second spring cleaning, the first having been done to neither her standards nor her specifications.

Sophie nodded and silently practiced saying no to Lionel half a dozen different ways. No, I merely teach the village children sums and reading, not what your sons need. No, the boys and I got off to a wretched start. No, my father relies on my assistance with his parishioners and his commentaries. No, I have my own life, a rich, fulfilling life, embracing good deeds, good friends, and good books.

The town respected her, and she respected herself.

So why was the prospect of working for Lionel so tempting?

It *couldn't* be her old obsession with him roaring back to life. Because it *couldn't* concern her if Lionel Westfall, Viscount Cordrey and love of her life, was home and free after twenty years.

She'd been over loving him for years.

"Try the lemon crème, Miss Bowerbank," Mrs. Plumridge prodded with stiff pride. "His Lordship stole our chef from Lord Weedon in London."

"Our magistrate *stole* his chef?" Sophie asked. She wouldn't put it past him. After all, he'd long ago stolen her heart, and everything but her virginity, and left her empty and aching and so compromised that she never married.

Never mind that his leaving had been no more his fault than hers. That he'd been dragged off under protest to a war he didn't want to fight and a risk of injury and death no man deserved.

"Very handy at the card table, His Lordship is," the house-keeper boasted, inappropriately, to Sophie's mind.

But the lemon crème was delicious. "Excellent, Mrs. Plumridge," she said, only nibbling the buttery frosted sweet, trying not to spoil her supper.

Trying not to be intimidated by the immaculate yellow drawing room where eminent guests were usually received. The housekeeper's nose pinched with disapproval. Clearly, she thought the rector's daughter had no business there.

Sophie didn't, and she knew it. Her station and her expectations—her most cherished hopes and dreams—were miles beneath this magnificence.

The room was luxurious. Its yellow damask curtains and brocade upholstery matched wall hangings of watered silk. In another life she would choose something very like this, but her life was the dark and dreary rectory. And she should be there now, seeing to her father's dinner.

To the devil with Lionel's power over her. She was not about to put an earl who'd forgotten her above a father who'd forgiven everything.

She set down the rich crème, half eaten. "I must be going, Mrs. Plumridge, truly. Papa will worry, which is not good for his heart."

The housekeeper huffed, plainly offended for her master. "His Lordship won't approve, Miss Bowerbank."

His Lordship can just choke on it, Sophie thought defiantly, but said, "Splendid tea, Mrs. Plumridge." At the door, she turned and gave the old bat her best smile. "His Lordship knows where to find me."

She hoped he wouldn't try. After that summer, month after month had passed. No word had come from him, and she'd put her childish dream of a life with Lionel Westfall behind her like another girl would pack away her dolls.

In time she'd accepted his silence. His duties to a father and an earldom outweighed a summer's passion for a penniless rector's daughter. He'd survived the war only to be sacrificed by his father at the tender age of twenty-one to that awful wife.

For Wraxham. For money.

And her heart had broken all over again. But that was twenty years ago, and she'd put that hurt behind her too and set about living a useful, exemplary life.

The south pasture edged the rectory's modest orchard, and Sophie took a narrow sheep's path across the field. Though short, it was her most private route to home, and the walk would help her compose her thoughts. A public grilling by His Lordship was tumult enough for one afternoon. It had been grueling, but gratifying. For he seemed to retain a fond memory or two of her, and he respected her intelligence.

Of course, she was flattered that the rakish, urbane Lionel Westfall had asked her to teach his sons.

In a perverse way, she was flattered that he needed her for anything.

In the most perverse way of all, she was flattered that he'd looked at her, almost as he'd done that summer.

Flattered? She'd been stunned. Thrilled.

Her feet flew along the footpath, her eyes fixed on the tiny indentations made by cloven hooves.

"Mind the gate, Miss Bowerbank."

It was Lionel's voice, urbane and ironic, and changed from the young man's baritone that had wooed her with light laughter and tender words. She looked ahead to see him standing at the kissing gate, that circular cage of a contraption where he'd snared her twenty years ago.

She no longer knew the man she had once loved. And still her heart thudded in her chest. His long, elegant hand rested on the gate's topmost curved iron bar, poised to open the gate and let her through.

Or trap her in it, as before. A thrill of anticipation coiled into her belly, shocking her into want . . . and wariness. Her body, if not her mind, was leaping to conclusions. Even if he might possibly still find her attractive, the reasons that had militated against them then still held. She had no money. No standing. No hope.

He was still handsome, but oh, the difference, she noticed with a little sense of loss. An immaculate town waistcoat of midnight superfine outlined his manly shoulders where once she'd seen and felt them beneath a simple linen shirt. It had been open at the neck where now a crisp white cravat framed his square, determined jaw. Skintight buff pants skimmed powerful, muscled legs and met gleaming Hessians at his knees. She missed the worn brown leather boots he'd worn when they had tromped together across fields.

Still, looking at a man like him was decidedly superior to thumbing through the old earl's erotic books, books she'd found last year in his library tucked behind some agricultural tracts on breeding sheep and managing marshland. At first they'd shocked her. Then, ever the student, she'd studied them in earnest, learning everything she could about the erotic passions that she'd missed. It couldn't matter that the sweetheart of her once-upon-a-summer's passion had become the object of her most private fantasies, the lover she imagined when she read the old earl's bawdy books. They were fantasies, merely fantasies, and Lionel was merely the only man she'd ever kissed.

Lionel's lazy gaze took a measure of her standing in the cool April twilight.

She looked back into his steely gray eyes, determined to give as good as she got. She could still feel. She too could still admire. She'd seen more of men's bodies in those old books than she'd ever seen of him, even a spectacularly fascinating etching that showed a man and his private parts. When she and Lionel had been young, she had touched him there but never dared to look.

She would dare now, she realized with a certain pride.

She would also dare to cross him. She forged into the cage of the gate, defying him to stop her.

Hinges creaked, and the hasp locked, and she was trapped

inside by the most devastatingly handsome man she had ever known.

Up close, his face had the same arrogant blade of a nose, but age had more sharply chiseled the angles of his cheeks and jaw. His tawny hair was cropped in the Byronic style that her friend Celia had raved over, but Sophie thought it made him look severe. A new scar split one brow. From that incident in the war, she thought with a chill, that had almost killed him. His well-shaped mouth turned down with a cynicism Sophie had never seen.

"You were to wait for me," he said, his gray eyes hard.

His reproof rubbed her wrong. She had waited once.

"You were very late."

"Which doesn't change the fact that I invited you to my home, and you saw fit to leave. Not a promising start to our new alliance."

"Your elevation to earl has dizzied your brain, my lord. I agreed to no alliance."

His face flushed. His eyes narrowed. "Then you will not agree to this."

Before she could suck in a breath of surprise, he lowered his head and sought her mouth. His lips were knowing, questing, and he pressed his tall frame to her breasts, radiating heat into her body. He deepened his kiss, his claim, and her head spun in amazement.

Twenty years of abstinence, of wondering and rectitude, and he was back, silky yet demanding, pushing her to respond to him.

He was every deep, dark, late-night fantasy of her spinsterish existence. Up till now, she had made him the golden lover of her fantasies, disembodied, safe.

The reality of him was better. Those bawdy books had not begun to capture what she'd missed—hot hands, humid breath, hard body. Her body awakened instantly, saluting her soul mate, acknowledging their old passion.

And suddenly the woman she'd grown into needed to know

if Lionel in the flesh could pleasure her as well as the Lionel of her dreams.

Sensation streaming through her veins, she parted her lips and met his teeth, and his tongue sought hers. He still smelled of musk and leather, tasted of exotic spices and smoky China tea. She was alive as she had been with him twenty years ago beside the stream, and since then, sometimes in the night, when her body quickened in the private place between her legs.

Sensations he had introduced her to.

But this was now, and waves of arousal settled in her belly, so urgent that she resented the iron gate that separated all but her mouth and arms and breasts from him, who must be, as she hoped and imagined, eager for her, hot and swollen . . .

How she regretted that they'd stopped those many years ago and left her intact. She circled an arm around his shoulders, ran her fingers up his hair, and she felt his hand seek out the shape of her breast and sculpt it with a gentle squeeze. She whimpered with desire.

He broke off the kiss with a disgusted oath.

Anger flared inside her. The nerve of the man, the arrogance, the decadence. To kiss her till her knees turned to pudding and not even pretend to care for her response. To use his rake's knowledge of women to melt her to her bones and spurn her when she yielded.

She should have been more guarded. She should have expected him to turn up changed.

Insulted to the toes of her thirty-five-year-old feet, she slapped his strong, square jaw.

Her hand made a red print on his sculpted jaw.

His sensuous mouth curved in a tight smile. "That settles that, Miss Bowerbank."

Her heart wobbled momentarily, but she said crisply, "That settles *what?*"

"That I can control myself around you, and if in a moment

of weakness I attempt the fortress of your charms, you can repel me."

She hadn't slapped him because he kissed her. She'd slapped him because he stopped. He found her old and unappealing.

She found him rude and cruel.

In her frostiest rector's daughter tone, she said, "Your storied London lovers did not change you for the better, my lord."

He gave a small cynical smile. "I shall have to change myself then."

She looked down at his hands, still trapping her inside the gate. "You might start with freeing me."

"Ah, yes. The gate," he said, as unruffled as if he ensnared gentlewomen of advancing age every day. Perhaps he did. He swung open the rounded bars and tucked her hand inside his arm. "I'll walk with you a way."

It was his gate, and these were his fields. She couldn't dredge up a single objection, except for the real ones. He'd made her want him, and she was angry that he could. Angry that she hadn't wanted him to stop.

She pulled her hand back from his clasp.

For years, in secrecy, she'd taken him to be her fantasy lover.

In reality, he was hotter and more exciting.

He just didn't think she was.

He adjusted his long stride to her shorter one, and they strolled together across his sheep pasture.

"My sons need a tutor, Miss Bowerbank," he began. They mounted the top of the last gentle down before her home.

"Or a drill sergeant, my lord," she quipped, her distraction driving her to make a smart retort.

He cut her a look, and his lazy gaze took a measure of her as . . . a woman? She was confused. Hadn't he just broken off their kiss?

"How badly they need a tutor, you have seen for yourself," he went on.

23

"But I am no tutor, my lord."

"A becoming modesty, Miss Bowerbank," he said, misinterpreting her objection. "But you have taught boys."

"Village boys only, my lord, and the few girls whose parents would allow it. Nothing that would prepare me to groom your sons for a serious course of study. Nothing whatsoever."

"Nothing, except years of your father's instruction and example. Adolphus Bowerbank is the most renowned scholar of our county."

She squirmed. He'd trapped her in his logic, as surely as he'd trapped her in the kissing gate. She couldn't deny her father's scholarly repute or his influence on her studies. She wouldn't lie and deny her qualifications.

"Your discipline," Lionel pointed out, "would benefit my sons as well."

She cocked her head, incredulous. "You cannot seriously expect me to manage those little hellions."

"Manage and instruct them, as you did this afternoon. The twins acknowledge you already. And my youngest, Simon—" Oddly, his voice faltered. "Simon . . . since his mother . . . he needs a softer hand."

She started to object.

But Lionel was looking over the gentle downs that now belonged to him, his shoulders slightly bent in sadness or despair. What troubled him? The memory of his wife? Or the mention of his youngest son?

Knee aching, Lionel minded his gait and collected his wits. At a woman's pace, he could hide his limp. But could he hide his passion? What the devil had possessed him to trap Sophie Bowerbank in the kissing gate? And then to claim that steamy kiss . . .

The rector's daughter was as lush and daring and unexpected as she'd been twenty years ago.

This afternoon in the grange hall, bringing her home to tutor his sons had seemed a stroke of genius. One crushing kiss

made it seem his rashest act since charging that fated horn-
works on a hill in France.

The rashest, but still smart, to hire her for his sons.

Her learning was as celebrated in the village as his rakehell
exploits were in town. It would take months and money to
find her like, and time and funds were at a premium at Wraxham House. He could contain his lusty leanings. She could
forgive his hasty, ill-considered kiss. He would persuade her
that she'd be safe from him at Wraxham House. Apart from
his unlamented wife, he'd grown very good at persuading
women.

"My sons just lost their mother," he began.

"I am deeply sorry for your loss, my lord," she said with more
sympathy than he needed or deserved.

"I just uprooted them from the only home they ever knew,"
he went on, his tone grave, "from a town filled with friends
and adventures to a strange, dull country place they scarcely
know. This afternoon's escapade . . . We're not off to a good
start in the village. The twins need help putting London behind
them."

She shook her head . . . but with understanding, he thought.
He hadn't lost his touch.

"I cannot stand in their mother's place," she said.

"Naturally," he agreed. "And yet, Simon is only seven, and
quite lost without her. He needs someone very like a mother."

"Surely his nurse—"

". . . Is new, and not a mother," he countered, more
smoothly than he felt. Simon's new nurse replaced a silly
young French woman, fashionable enough for Penelope's
taste but not dependable enough for Lionel's requirements.
He needed someone who could do what he could not.

"I would be new, and not a mother."

"You would be dependable."

"You are not listening, my lord. I lack experience."

"You have never taught ones so young," he observed, not
asking.

"Only little ones at church. I thought you wanted me for the older boys."

"And for Simon. He is quite bright, and very much alone."

Her warm brown eyes widened in compassion, but she said only, "A sad story, my lord."

He took out his snuffbox, a peer's best refuge in domestic plights. "He needs only a bit of sums and spelling, while the older boys work at their desks."

"Indeed, my lord," she said, agreeing to nothing. But she just needed another push, he sensed it in her tone.

"You will help us out then."

"I have my father's health and welfare to consider."

"Of course. I trust he's well." He dipped an ornate silver ladle in the spicy snuff, its complex smell evoking London even here, hobbling along in the earthy country air.

"Well but aging, overworked," she said.

He remembered the man from years ago, a thoughtful scholar and avid collector of antique and modern books for his studies on the mystery plays.

He'd also been an advocate for bright young men . . . Lionel included, until he'd caught Lionel with his too-young daughter in a compromising state of near undress. The rector and the earl had concurred on exiling Lionel to war, speedily and irrevocably.

Lionel had protested violently, but his father vowed to ruin the rector—and his daughter—unless Lionel complied. Furious that his father had all the power, he'd thrown himself into war.

"Your father always did spend hours at his commentaries," he said blandly.

Her green eyes darkened in the twilight, scheming. "Indeed, my lord, but he overworks himself on your behalf."

"On my behalf," he repeated carefully. Sophie never used to scheme.

She pressed her lips together, obviously a little miffed she hadn't gotten a rise out of him. "Since your father first appointed him, my father has strained his eyesight and wrecked his health for your household and your tenants."

The appointment had been his father's, not his, Lionel wanted to say. But he was earl now, heir to more obligations than privileges. "Your father has been most dedicated."

"My father has grown old and is no longer well." She drew herself up, as bold in defending her father as in accusing Lionel's sons. "He's too frail for circuits, sick calls, and funerals in the rain. Bring in a vigorous young vicar to handle his more strenuous duties . . . and I might consider your offer."

Bugger all. The crowd's respect for her at Upton Grange was well earned. Daring young Sophie had grown into a woman with ideas, more than usual in a woman of her class. It became her, except that a streak of independent thinking did not bode well for his needs or his control.

Nevertheless, for his sons' sakes, he was prepared to take the bull by the horns, or rather, to call the gentlewoman on her bluff.

He stopped and palmed his enameled box. "Let us frame that another way," he said as if at leisure. "The moment you've established yourself at Wraxham House as my sons' tutor, I will find your father an earnest, obsequious young vicar to order about."

"Lionel!" she admonished, then clapped her hand over her mouth.

He should not be pleased to hear his given name roll off her tongue as if twenty years had never passed. But they had passed, and he barely remembered the young man she'd known. She might have stayed home with her father, but he'd become the earl, her father's benefactor, with power to elevate or lower, dismiss or restore.

Recovering, she said acidly, "You cannot threaten my father, my lord. That's bribery."

He gave his faint smile, the one that worked in London when he was in dire straits. "I could throw in a better salary for my tutor. If she needs it."

27

"You well know we need it. He hasn't changed one whit since your schoolboy days. Generous to a fault with his parishioners . . . and profligate in buying books to annotate his blasted commentaries."

"His choice . . ." Lionel offered.

"His weakness." She bit her lip, her tender kissable lip, and added, "You have snared me well and truly."

Her words sent all the wrong messages to his wayward brain and determined privates.

"And the salary, my lord?" she went on.

"The usual. Tims, my secretary, handles that."

She gave him a truly annoying, upright, rector's daughter's look of disapproval. "I don't suppose an earl concerns himself with the details of his sons' lives."

But he did. He'd spent these last weeks making up for years he'd lost. And he knew what Penelope paid for tutors. "Ordinarily, it's thirty pounds a year."

Sophie shook her head. "Those are a governess's wages, not a tutor's fee. I should think sixty would insure a quality of instruction."

Spot on, he thought ruefully. He'd failed his sons inexcusably by leaving such matters to his wife. Perhaps the paltry salaries explained the endless parade of London tutors. A false economy, instituted by his wife and implemented by his secretary.

On the other hand, surely a teacher in the provinces was put to less expense than one who lived in town.

But he didn't want to seem mean. "Forty pounds, then."

"That's not four pounds a month," Sophie objected.

"If you last a month, we can revisit the matter."

That got her back up. She resumed their walk, striding decisively around a copse of elms and yews. His bad knee ground on itself, but he soldiered on, surprisingly at ease with the objecting Sophie, the opinionated Sophie, the stubborn Sophie.

The rectory came into distant view.

"If you make it worth my while to come, my lord, I will last as long as I am needed."

Greedy wench. "Fifty pounds, then."

Perhaps women were always greedy, he thought, but swatted that notion away. Penelope had been born to greed, and courtesans squirreled away their pence for their old age. But Sophie's stated goal was to serve her father.

"Sixty," she persisted.

"Sixty?" For a woman?

"You do want me to be responsible for three boys, my lord."

He had negotiated more effectively with courtesans over a new suite. "I insist on it," he said.

She did not appear impressed. "So, sixty pounds, for the older boys' instruction in Latin, rhetoric, history, geography, and a smattering of Italian and French. Reading and sums for Simon, with any of the foregoing subjects added as soon as he is ready. Am I right?"

"A high price for nothing more than the usual courses of study."

"You forget that my father will have to pay someone to do the copying and other work I ordinarily do for him."

Lionel was torn between admiration and annoyance. His wayward boys deserved that exasperating persistence. For her to nag him was another matter altogether.

"Fifty will compensate you for your time and some village woman for her trouble."

"And for my trouble? What is that worth to you, my lord?"

He pressed his lips together. Parted them to concede, "Sixty it is, then, Miss Bowerbank."

It was a great deal of money for a woman from the provinces, taking on her first serious students, and students from a great house. He expected courtesy, even gratitude, to meet his generous concession.

"You will begin tomorrow."

"Monday, if you please, my lord," she said, aping his civility. "I cannot instantly put aside my obligations."

"Of course," he conceded. He could afford to yield on this.

So he was taken aback when she continued, "I will require free rein, just as I had with my village pupils."

He arched his scarred brow. "Free rein as to what exactly?"

"Assignments, penalties, and punishments," she asserted.

"Very well, Miss Bowerbank," he said, uncomfortable in allowing her control. But she was not Penelope, taking charge, bargaining with her money and her sex to usurp a husband's usual command. Sophie was only asking what tutors normally got. "Free rein, short of bullwhips and iron shackles."

"I will tolerate no parental prompting, no fatherly meddling."

"I do not interfere with tutors," he said curtly. "Except to evaluate their monthly reports."

Her face clouded. "My consent is contingent, my lord, upon one further thing."

"Yes, Miss Bowerbank?"

Her green eyes dared him to deny her. "There will be no further ambushes of a sensual nature in the kissing gate or elsewhere."

So what if it had been a bit of an ambush, born of exasperation that she hadn't waited for him, and a mild curiosity he was unwilling to examine? She'd enjoyed every moment of his advances, he'd stake his favorite phaeton on it. He would not, however, indulge another such embrace.

"Quite right, Miss Bower—"

"It wouldn't be proper, as I'm sure you agree, for students to see their tutor kissing their father in their own home. And your advances will not sit well with me."

The gentle green pasture rose and fell around them, and damp earth smells rising reminded him of heartfelt kisses and steamy embraces many years ago. He couldn't resist. He put out a hand to end her lecture and tipped her chin.

"Recent evidence to the contrary, Sophie," he said softly.

Her mouth made a round O of dismay, and tears of mortification sprang to her shocked green eyes. "I made a mistake," she whispered. "It will not happen again."

She was wary of him, arms stiff as starch at her sides. It was not her best pose, and it wouldn't wash at Almack's. But her resistance sent a rush of interest pulsing through him. Interest he was squelching, now.

He'd come here to rusticate, not fornicate.

Nevertheless, he thought grimly, apart from monitoring her—in the schoolroom, with his sons present—he was going to have to keep very, very busy after Sophie Bowerbank moved into his home.

Chapter Three

Our eyes each other's charms review . . .
—The Pleasures of Coition (1721)

The schoolroom clock at Wraxham House clanged a dark metallic warning. Standing behind her desk, Sophie gave her sober muslin frock a furtive swipe, more to smooth her nerves than any wrinkles. She'd always embraced challenges, hadn't she? She was a pea goose, fretting over the change.

She had a challenge now. It was seven o'clock in the morning, and her charges were late. Long moments ticked worryingly by.

The more worrying as she was being watched. Judged.

Beside a screen at the back of the schoolroom, Lionel sat on a too-small chair, one leg bent, the other stretched out, long and muscled. What had happened to their agreement? *No parental prompting, no fatherly meddling.*

Equally as bad, what had happened to him? Short though it was, his tawny hair was disturbingly tousled so early in the morning, and mud caked his tall black boots. He must have had a morning ride. Or a late-night frolic at Tobias Jolly's inn, the Wraxham Arms.

Her heart pinched, and she chided herself for thinking like a gossip. And yet, Lionel had come home with such a reputation. An earned one, judging from his coolly sophisticated air and his hot, devastating kiss. Would Wraxham's new earl and magistrate turn back to rake at night? Would his sons turn up at all?

What could she have been thinking to consent to this?

With relief she heard the clatter of running feet. The door burst open, and the Honorable Masters Maxim and Alexander Westfall caromed in, dodging desks, chairs, bookstands, chalkboards, and a precariously mounted globe. Bumping each other smack in front of her, the sturdy twins slapped grammars on their desks. The books landed, Sophie noted, at the exact same insolent angle.

They offered innocent smiles.

Her heart squeezed. Lionel's towheaded sons, scrubbed and flushed, were choirboy beautiful, their round, sun-kissed faces just at the age before burgeoning manhood would stamp them with harsher features.

She was not deceived. "Good morning, gentlemen. Or rather, since you have yet to earn that honor, boys. Let's do that again please. Properly, this time."

Max scowled in confusion, but Alex bridled. She ignored both reactions while Lionel looked on. She braced herself against whatever criticism he might be storing up and said in her most matter-of-fact manner, "There is a proper way to enter my schoolroom. At a walk, and in a straight line. Take a stand beside your desk, with your book in your hand at your side. Then in an extremely courteous tone of voice, you say to me, 'Good morning, Miss Bowerbank.' And I will answer, 'Good morning, Max. Good morning, Alex.'"

Alex blurted, "Why is it always him first?"

"Because I put him first," she said, cutting off his impertinence. "Then I say, 'How are you this morning?' And you an-

33

swer, 'Very well, Miss Bowerbank, thank you.' And you sit down, mindful to place your books quietly on the desk."

The twins exchanged conspiratorial glances, and Max asked, "What if it slips?"

Oh dear. Stopping them from tossing stones had been easier than wrangling over manners, and on her first day, and in front of Lionel. But she wouldn't let his scrutiny dash her confidence or compromise her command.

"Poor boy," she said to Max with false solicitude. "Is it too heavy for you?"

Max colored. "No, Miss Bowerbank. I can manage."

"Walk to the back of the room then, and enter again, properly this time. I'm sure two bright young men can perform that simple task."

Max complied, but Alex balked.

"Both of you. Now. I keep the cat-o'-nine-tails right behind the desk," she pressed on, assuring herself that she could butt heads as solidly with the spoiled sons of aristocrats as with village waifs.

They gawked in disbelief . . . then smothered approving grins. A cat-o'-nine-tails, as she'd hoped, bespoke familiarity with naval exploits and possibly even pirate lore. With a shuffle and a flurry, they marched to the back of the room and straight back to their desks, matching boys with matching walks and matching tousled straw-blond hair. Facing her, they delivered their morning greetings, letter perfect and polite. She allowed herself to let out a pent-up breath of relief. Her strategy had worked, for now.

Then she glanced over to the screen. Her critic had slipped out, leaving her to her own devices with his little devils. Had he approved, or not?

Her chalk had moved again. She had stepped to the window to draw a curtain against the afternoon sun, and returned to find her chalk no longer in its cradle beneath the slate board. It could not have moved itself.

She rummaged on her desk. There it was, alongside her prized dictionary she'd brought along from home.

But for the third time this morning, when the chalk disappeared, she'd not heard a sound, neither when she turned to poke the fire, nor when she walked across the room to hang up her shawl. Not so much as a smirk or snicker had betrayed Lionel's little devils.

In spite of their tricks and subversions, they had to be good boys at heart: They stood by each other. They were not bad students either. Max could multiply long numbers in his head while Alex declined his Latin nouns and conjugated verbs adeptly. Despite their pranks, they seemed willing to learn. But perhaps their bursts of compliance were only owing to their father's intrusive presence.

He had dropped by the schoolroom half a dozen times, as if doubting her competence until he saw it for himself. Or perhaps he merely stopped to see her, for his iron-gray eyes studied her every move. Her stomach did a little somersault.

She pocketed her chalk, resolved to remove the boys' temptation. But what to do about hers?

Lionel sat on the too-short chair again, his long muscular legs stretched before him, his gaze intent—on her. When she faced the boys, his eyes went from her bosom to her mouth and back. When she faced the slate board, she imagined his attention burning a trail up and down her spine.

Which pleased her, and disturbed her. But she determined not to let him intimidate her. While the boys copied out their lessons, she assessed him in return. This older Lionel was fuller, darker, more urbane, any trace of the idealistic, gentle youth she'd loved lost to city pleasures. Lines of age—or dissolution, if she could believe the rumors—scored his once smooth brow and creased the corners of his once gentle mouth.

Cynical now, but still so kissable.

Blast! She was a woman grown, and hardly innocent, but it would never do to entertain such fantasies in front of Lionel and his sons. Tamping down her sensual thoughts, Sophie forged on to the geography of the Levant and slammed into a wall of ignorance. By the time she'd breached it and looked up again, Lionel was gone.

At last the long day ended. Relieved, she packed her portfolio, snatched up her chip straw bonnet, and bolted for the door. Her first day of tutoring had not been a disaster. In fact, she felt rather competent, sure she had done Lionel's twins some good. Over luncheon with them, she'd met his youngest son, the highlight of her day. Simon was a shy seven-year-old, his soft brown hair framing soulful chocolate eyes that exuded loneliness and loss. Afterward she spent an hour with him doing sums and quietly reading while his brothers tackled their first Cicero.

Tomorrow she'd come better prepared to help the poor little tyke. For now she was late for seeing Papa's dinner on the table. She hurried past the tapestries and paintings lining Wraxham's upper hallway, down two broad flights of stairs, and onto the gleaming black and white marble foyer.

Decidedly masculine footsteps overtook her.

"Where do you think you're going, Miss Bowerbank?"

Confused, she stopped and turned. His Lordship loomed above her, city-sleek in black for dinner, and censorious.

"Home to my father, naturally, my lord."

"My sons' tutors reside in our home."

Odd, she thought, that Wraxham House seemed like home to him. Odder, that he expected her to stay. "You failed to mention residence when we set our terms."

"You are to establish yourself at Wraxham House."

"You asked only that I establish myself in your schoolroom."

"At sixty pounds, you will fulfill the duties of our regular tutors."

"But I am not a regular tutor, my lord."

"Even so, you will stay and sleep here."

Her heart thumped at the prospect. "I am sorry, my lord, but I did not agree to sleep with you."

36

One corner of his mouth crooked.

Blast. Had she said *sleep with him?* And betrayed exactly what was on her mind. "I mean, sleep here . . . I mean, at Wraxham House. I mean, overnight," she stammered, and then blurted in exasperation, "Don't you see? A spinster living unprotected under your roof would instantly excite notions of the most improper behavior."

"I'm certain the rector's daughter would bring propriety to any situation."

She didn't see how, not with this new and inconvenient hunger for him coursing through her veins. How could she be so foolish? So wanton? Even at this very instant, his steely, piercing eyes, his knowing lips, his long, surprising hands . . . Her mouth went dry. Her knees went weak. He was so close, so elegant, and so much more desirable than in her fantasies.

"My father expects me, my lord. Depends on me."

"Come, come, Miss Bowerbank," he chided in his superior manner. "The boys will soon depend on you, too, for reading after supper and tucking into bed."

"Tucking into bed?"

"It is good to read to children, is it not?" he asked, as if treading new ground.

"Indeed, but should you not do that yourself?"

"I will not always be here. Simon needs—" Lionel's face shadowed, concealing . . . What more could the poor child need than his father's love? "—My youngest son will require you in the evenings even more. You won't have time for to-ing and fro-ing."

"I never to and fro, my lord. I help my father with his parishioners and his commentaries. We have put my past behind us, and I owe him everything."

Lionel's eyes flashed with something like resentment, then shuttered. "Very well. Go home tonight. Tomorrow, and every night thereafter, you will dine with my sons and me, and then stay the night in your own chambers here."

She drew on wounded pride—old wounds, new pride—

and harrumphed in rebellion. "Once the boys are in bed, I fail to see what difference my presence could make."

His brow furrowed momentarily as if she might have a point, or he might have a reason, but he threatened smoothly, "You would do well to remember: I can still put your father out to pasture."

Disappointment swept her. "You've changed, my lord. The Lionel I once knew never bullied women, especially not those below his station."

He didn't bother to deny that her station was below his. "The Lionel you once knew did not have six sons at the brink of savagery, madam. They require your presence here. I require it."

"I shall think over your irresistible offer, my lord, and send word tomorrow if I cannot meet your terms," she said briskly, knowing that she would oblige him in the end.

He gave a stiff bow, obviously displeased that she'd not instantly deferred to his demand. A tall, gaunt liveried footman showed her out the door and, under Lionel's orders, followed her home in the fading light. As if she needed protection. It was just another show of Lionel's rank and power, unnecessary and unwanted. She'd grown up walking all over her safe quiet village and Wraxham's surrounding fields. No one, nothing, would be afoot tonight.

Nothing but her tumbling thoughts, as she crossed the dew-drenched downs. What was she to do? She'd believed she was over Lionel, past railing against his superior class, beyond lamenting her own inferior charms.

But her nighttime fantasies of him had left her dangerously attuned to the actual attractions she had seen these last few days—the curl of his tawny, Byronic hair, the rakish scar that marred one perfect eyebrow, the intriguing bulge at the join of his muscled legs.

Dangerously attuned, and vulnerable to wild imaginings.

Kissing Lionel again reminded her too painfully what she'd gone on to renounce: love, marriage, children, even the possibility of passion—all, on a point of honor. Lionel had not ruined her in fact, but she knew too much. She could never have pretended innocence. She'd given him her heart.

And she would not deny a prospective spouse his right to her whole heart or his right to take an innocent woman to his marriage bed.

She unlocked the rectory's gate and crossed the flagstone path to her father's house.

Her summer's affair with Lionel had taught her everything she knew of the ways of a woman with a man. That, and what she'd since learned from his father's books. Now the idealistic, bookish lad whom she remembered, whom she had *loved,* was lost behind a veneer of style and sophistication, a consequence no doubt of the war and his years in London with his ambitious wife.

Perhaps that lad was lost forever.

How ironic that she found the man even more compelling than the lad. Did she dare take up Lionel's offer and go live alongside him, subjected daily, perhaps hourly, to his appeal? Tantalized . . . but never to be satisfied. For Lionel—the recently widowed, newly titled, aristocratic Lionel—had tested her temptations at his first opportunity and turned away. Small comfort to imagine he'd turned away from her because he was grieving his late wife. Everyone knew he wasn't.

Sophie opened the back door on a bite of misery. She could move to his house, teach his twins, and comfort his youngest son. His sons might need her, but she wanted him, wanted him to teach her what other women, whether wives or mistresses or bawds, knew of men. Could she bear to live and work in his presence every day, older, frumpier, wanting him, wanting kisses he wouldn't offer, caresses he wouldn't give?

With luck, her father—the repository of spiritual insight, after all—would bring his wisdom to bear on her predicament. With luck, he would give her the grounds she needed to decline Lionel's offer. And a way around Lionel's threat to his position.

Chapter Four

Ne'er shall I forget the hour,
When to the lone, sequester'd bow'r,
To meet my love I stole . . .
—The Temple of Prostitution (1779)

"It's a scandalous offer, Papa," Sophie forced herself to point out that evening after dinner.

Scandalous, and far too tempting, but surely she could count on her father to save her from herself.

His bespectacled eyes assessed her over his evening reading. He was over sixty now, white-haired and thin. "You worked in his father's library happily enough these last . . . How many years did Wraxham employ you?"

"Three and a half, Papa, but I came home every night."

"Ah, yes, so you did." He thumbed the pages of his latest extravagant addition to his library, reluctant to put it down. "Are you saying you're not interested, Sophia? It isn't like you to turn away where there are children in need."

"Boys, Papa. Rapscallions I am ill prepared to manage."

"Evidently our new earl disagrees. The village is abuzz over how well you handled the twins in the matter of the Misses Gatewoods' sheets."

"That was an incident, not a course of instruction."

" 'Twas handsomely done, my love. Everyone on the vestry committee commended you to me for your vigilance. His Lordship merely salutes your superior abilities and wishes to give your learning full play."

"No, he demands that I take up residence at Wraxham House. That is the sticking point. I may no longer be a green girl, but I cannot stay there unchaperoned. He cannot expect it, and you should not allow it."

"I would chaperone you myself, my love, but for my duties to my flock." With a sigh, he marked his place with scholarly precision and closed the leather volume. "I should like nothing better than to have a turn at Wraxham's famous collections."

Her father was hopelessly addicted to his books. "You have quite a collection of your own, Papa."

"But never the means to expand it as I wish. It pained me beyond words to pass up that book Horton brought by last week."

She'd seen the illustrated fifteenth-century *Book of Hours*, done by hand in gold leaf and brilliant inks. It was exceedingly rare, obscenely expensive, and as seductive to her father as Lionel Westfall was to her.

"For heaven's sake, Papa! The man wanted forty guineas."

"I'm sure 'twas worth sixty." Her father rubbed his ink-stained hands at the thought of such a treasure.

"You've never made money buying and selling books," she reminded him as kindly as she could.

"I could have traded it and used the twenty pounds' profit to pay down my little debt to Wraxham," he said stubbornly.

Little debt. Bah. The twenty pounds he'd never see was a fraction of his total indebtedness, she'd bet on it.

"Chances are good, Papa, that you wouldn't have parted

41

with it at any price. Which is what landed you in such a sorry state. Too many books, too little money."

His hand caressed the morocco binding of his abandoned book, and his eyes narrowed. "Wraxham offers to pay you, does he not?"

"Yes, Papa. Sixty pounds a year."

"Sixty pounds!" He frowned skeptically. "For a woman?"

"Yes, Papa."

"Handsome of him . . . very handsome, my love," he sputtered, then said, "I don't see how we can say no to such a respectable offer. It would greatly help to defray our household expenses."

"Rubbish, Papa. You'll spend it straightaway on books."

"Now, Sophie, you know I—"

"I know you're as bad as an opium eater when it comes to parchment, vellum, and gold-tipped lettering. I should think a man in your position would consider His Lordship's reputation, to say nothing of my own."

The Right Reverend Adolphus Bowerbank focused on the papers before him, probably a Sunday sermon exhorting his flock to be kind to one another.

"Well, my love," he said after long moments, "your little indiscretion with him was many years ago. We've put it behind us, haven't we? Forgiven and forgotten, and gone on about our lives."

It hadn't been that simple. After the old earl had banished Lionel, Sophie's father had sent her to his sister's by the sea for a couple of months. "To heal her broken heart," he'd said. Years later as she'd learned more about womanly matters, she'd realized that he'd sent her there in case she turned up with child.

So his about-face stunned her, and the truth struck her like the apostle Paul's vision on the road to Damascus, clear and inescapable.

"Just how much money are we owing, Papa?"

"I, well . . ." he began, then crumpled under the weight of

his fiscal indiscretion. "At that rate, 'twould take you ten years to repay Wraxham's note against me."

"Six hundred pounds!" she exploded. "Heavenly days! Does His Lordship know?"

"I'm sure the new earl has more important financial concerns before him than my modest debt."

"Modest to him perhaps. He must deal in hundreds, even thousands of pounds a day. But there is nothing modest about a debt that would take me ten years of work to repay. This is shameful. Really, Papa, I am speechless."

"On the contrary, Sophia, you have rather too much to say to an old man," Adolphus Bowerbank admonished, his tired eyes wounded above his thick round spectacles. "My books are godly books, tools I need to write my commentaries."

Godly books. The notion tweaked her conscience. She had hardly taken the high moral road herself. The bawdy books she'd borrowed from Wraxham's library were far from godly, were godforsaken, some might say. And they obsessed her. Nevertheless, she enjoyed her fantasies while reading borrowed books, not purchased ones, and her father's expenses were hard reality.

"The harm is not in your books, Papa. It is in your inability to resist them. Debt compromises you. And now it compromises me."

Surely he could see that. A soft spring light cast a golden glow over the rectory's narrow dining room, but the three small logs they'd lit for warmth barely cut the April chill. They restored their usual harmony by moving on to safer subjects, Juvenalian satire versus the Horatian style, only to be interrupted, halfway through a disputed point, by a ladylike tapping at the door.

Sophie snapped her book shut. "Oh dear, it must be Celia. I almost forgot. It's poetry night, and we meet at the Misses Gatewoods' house."

Eyes brimming with gossip, Celia swooped in to pay her

43

regards and to verify her latest scoop with that reliable source the rector.

"Am I to understand, Reverend Bowerbank, that our Sophie is to have the honor of educating Wraxham's sons?"

Sophie's father looked of two minds. " 'Tis a vexed affair, Miss Upton, which we were just discussing. Wraxham engaged her to do just that. But he adds a problematical condition— that she reside at Wraxham House. Sophia is reluctant to move in with a known rake—that is, a widower, unchaperoned."

Celia's fashionable blond curls bobbed agreement. "Ah. Difficult, indeed. But a suitable companion, sir, should not be that hard to—"

"A companion . . ." Sophie's father mused, taking off his glasses and twiddling them in the air.

Then his and Celia's gazes caught and held, and Sophie had the sense of inevitable forces conspiring against her.

Or for her? She could not be sure.

"You don't happen to be free during the next few weeks, Miss Upton, until we could find someone . . ."

"Older, perhaps, someone less engaged socially than I am at times? Quite right. A needy gentlewoman, who would serve, and be served, by the task."

Celia paused dramatically, and Sophie felt a ripple of irritation with her very oldest friend. She was milking the moment, self-aggrandizing prima donna that she could sometimes be.

"Naturally, Papa, we wouldn't want to burden Celia with such a constraining position." She turned to her friend. "You have so many more pressing engagements than we are used to."

Celia sniffed in contradiction. "My present pressing engagement is my father's convalescence, Sophie, and my sisters have that well in hand. They can spare me a few weeks."

"It would be awfully tedious, entertaining yourself while I'm engaged hours on end in the schoolroom," Sophie objected.

But why did she object? Her father needed money. She

wanted work. She even wanted to be near Lionel, ninny that she was. And yet, did she want her friend Celia with her in Lionel's house?

Of course she did. Their friendship had weathered worse than this. Ages ago they'd managed to stay friends after Celia's choice of suitor had—through no encouragement from Sophie—proposed to Sophie first. At least he'd accepted Sophie's refusal after going off to war, and from Spain had sent Celia a token ring. He'd been the last opportunity either of them had had to marry. After he was killed, Sophie had mourned the man, and Celia had mourned the marriage that would never be.

"With the many amenities of Wraxham House at my disposal, I believe I can entertain myself," Celia said, with a graceful yet dramatic wave of the hand that still wore Ewan Ramsay's ring. "I might even read a book."

"You're a tireless reader—"

"Precisely, dearest, I can amuse myself. And besides, His Lordship will undoubtedly have company. Who knows what . . . opportunities might present themselves for new connections of consequence? While in London, he traveled in the highest circles."

It was not Celia's best trait, Sophie thought, this ambition to place herself among her betters, but her offer was a generous one.

"How very kind of you to accommodate us, Miss Upton," Sophie's father said, letting out a breath. "I'm certain our Sophia—upon reflection—will be happy for you to join her."

"It isn't that I won't be happy, Papa," Sophie said. "But there's more to this than meets the eye."

A very great deal more, now that the tables were turned and she could not rely on her father for an excuse not to go. If her response to Lionel's kiss was any indication of her weakness, she had everything to lose: her father's good opinion, her reputation, and her heart.

Because living practically in Lionel's pocket would be torture, no matter how much stronger she was than the young girl who'd loved him heart and soul. Even if he proved indifferent to her, she was falling for him all over again, and falling fast, at considerable risk to her cherished independence and hard-won self-respect.

"Of course, my love," her father went on, "there always is. Why, only consider those poor boys. Mrs. Plumridge says the youngest screams in his sleep at night."

Oh, dear heavens! Lionel had hinted at a problem with the little tyke, but nothing so disturbing as that. Sophie felt a pull of sympathy for the child and for the father. And yet . . .

"I meant . . ." She couldn't be explicit. ". . . about the past."

Celia, ever attuned to juicy scandal, perked up. "The past? Whose past? His Lordship's?"

Sophie's father hemmed and hawed, then ducked behind his oracular minister's voice. "We all have pasts, my dears, and 'tis our Christian duty to repent, put them behind us, and go on to do right. Whatever your scruples are, Sophia love, they cannot bear more weight than the needs of those poor orphaned boys."

Poor! Sophie spluttered inwardly. Scions of wealth and consequence, who needed her slim talents like a sail needs a lady's fan to fill it. Leave it to her father's philosophic turn of mind to rationalize a good reason for her to go to Wraxham House. Which seemed inevitable now.

For between Lionel's authority, her father's financial foibles, and Celia's too-convenient offer, she was well and truly trapped.

She lifted her hands in surrender. "Very well then, Papa, Celia. His Lordship orders me not to miss another night. I can pack after our meeting, and move in tomorrow morning."

"Brava, daughter!" her father said, doubtless relieved about his debts and heedless of the danger to her heart.

She turned to her friend. "Celia, can you possibly pack and move in, in time to join us for dinner?"

Celia sputtered. She needed new gowns to stay at Wraxham

House. Sophie suggested ordering them after Celia settled in. Surely she could not want Sophie to spend one night alone at Wraxham House, at the mercy of His Lordship, noted London rake.

Celia promised to pull herself together and pack for the momentous move.

But that evening at the Misses Gatewoods', Celia's attention to the much admired *Elegiac Sonnets* of Mrs. Charlotte Smith was intermittent and distracted.

In the rectory, near midnight, Sophie started packing, filling her father's ancient battered trunk with her own favorite texts. At least, at last, she had a way to return the old earl's bawdy books she'd still had at home the night he died. She buried them amidst the scholarly tomes, and turned to her few dresses.

Her spirits sank with each worn frock she laid on her bed and examined for repairs. She had only one good silk dress for evenings, and it was frayed and out of fashion. She folded it atop the books along with her three muslin day dresses, worrying.

Tomorrow night she would be living under the same roof with the only man she'd ever loved. The only man who'd ever touched and fondled her in her most secret, private places. The only man she wanted.

She could still say no.

She should say no.

She might deceive her father that she would be working to pay back his old debts or that she couldn't resist going to help the children.

She would not lie to herself. Remnants of the daring romantic lass she'd been that summer fluttered back to life. Because she knew, as clear as St. Philip's bells on a sunny Sunday morning, that Lionel had felt a spark. Years ago, their fathers had abruptly and brutally ended their affair. But what if hers and Lionel's attraction to one another had survived the years?

She thought about that exhilarating kiss, again at the kissing gate. He'd vowed to avoid her, but she was sure their kiss had affected him too. He'd returned to the schoolroom to study her with an intensity that spoke of long embraces, wet hot kisses, and steamy lingering nights.

Hope rippled through her.

She had to find out if Lionel still cared. And she never would, staying here, in her safe but solitary bed.

She locked her trunk, fixing her resolve. Why not take a chance? Until this afternoon, she hadn't been kissed in almost twenty years. She wasn't getting any younger.

And a sterling reputation—or so the old earl's bawdy books suggested, and her own experience bore out—was a poor bedfellow, at best.

For Celia to come along as chaperone was a stroke of genius. Her presence could give Sophie the cover to explore her dreams and just perhaps fulfill her fantasies. If all else failed, Sophie might still be able to shed her troublesome virginity.

Chapter Five

"Oh grant again the am'rous bliss—
"The frantic, joyous, mad distress,
"The tumult of desire!"
—The Temple of Prostitution (1779)

Alone the next morning, Lionel spurned his usual leisurely breakfast of chocolate and rusk. He was a working earl now, with an estate to manage and debts to pay. He piled his plate with hearty country fare: broiled haddock, ham, and eggs.

He needed sustenance. Simon had had a terrible night, waking in the early morning hours from a nightmare of monsters tormenting his lost mother, keeping her from coming home. The boy's chambermaid had called Lionel to his side, and Lionel, besieged by memories of his own, had failed again to help his son. Inconsolable, Simon had not fallen asleep until dawn.

Lionel had not slept at all.

On top of that, Sophie was nowhere to be seen, and it was time for the twins' morning lessons. If ever they needed her, it was now, but she'd not sent one word from the rectory of her intentions.

Lionel glared at the cold dead haddock, the fresh-killed pig on his plate, feeling murderous. Sophie had to come. Yesterday he'd looked into his father's records and discovered the reverend's debt of several hundred pounds. If worse came to worst, and she didn't come to help his sons, Lionel was prepared to coerce her using that.

The door to the morning room creaked open, and Barnaby Tims, his efficient secretary, crept in, massive ledgers in his arms. "Beg pardon, my lord. But I was up until all hours correcting these for your perusal."

Lionel groaned inwardly. If Tims had been up, he'd bloody well have heard poor Simon screaming. Fresh fodder for household gossip—and at his son's cost—was not the best start for Lionel's new rule as earl.

Neither was letting his secretary set the agenda for his day. "Tomorrow, Tims. Set them there." He nodded toward the sideboard, laden with enough meats and pastries to feed a houseful of weekend guests.

Tims cleared his throat, Adam's apple bobbing. "Beg pardon, my lord. But the bank's representative is down from London today. He must have your imprimatur."

Lionel stabbed a sausage. "Did you correct the errors I found yesterday?"

"Yes, my lord."

"Did you introduce new ones?"

"N-no, my lord. I checked everything twice."

"Barns and fences are past repairs." An urgent task Lionel had put off until his sons were settled with a tutor, and would have put off again today if Sophie had not agreed to resume her post. "This morning I go out with Carter to meet with tenants about them."

Tims's thin lips primmed at the mention of his former assistant. Lionel had just elevated Carter, more expert in agricultural matters, over Tims, who resented it mightily but persisted,

"If you would just give these accounts one last perusal, my lord, the second mortgage depends upon my correctness and your concurrence."

Pedantic twit. Lionel broke off a chunk of haddock, and let the ledgers lie where Tims had placed them.

"I shall retrieve them, my lord, after you have breakfasted," Tims whispered, bowing and backing from the room.

Lionel rubbed fatigue from his eyes, to no avail. He was stuck with his father's staff. They knew too much about the workings of his complex estate for him to let them go. He forced his attention to the ledgers, a neat piece of work but as welcome over breakfast as pig's trotters. Outside, a cart rattled over the cobblestones paving Wraxham's back entrance.

That must be Sophie moving in. He felt a lightening of his spirits he could ill afford. But he'd watched her with his boys. Her competence would make all the difference. He was sure it would. He got up, walked to the window, and parted the draperies with the back of his hand to watch the unloading of her trunks.

Correct that, of her *trunk*. She'd brought only one. Penelope had required two for a weekend. Just how long did Sophie plan to stay? Perhaps he had not made himself clear or given her enough time to pack. More likely, she planned to stay only a short while. With luck, the twins would behave, and little Simon's plight would appeal to her sympathetic nature.

Bugger all. He was torturing himself like a besotted schoolboy. Sophie had one trunk because she was poor and had few things. She would stay because her overworked father needed the vice-vicar Lionel had promised. She would stay to pay her father's debts.

She would stay because the earl of Wraxham said so.

He allowed himself to admire her, sitting atop the borrowed oxcart in that cursed gray frock, a bookish and indomitable air about her, which she would bloody well need. That, and a sympathetic nature to help her deal with Simon. Given his misery last night, she was moving in not a moment too soon.

Not that he had prepared her for the gravity of his youngest son's disturbances. Perhaps no one could help. But her dealings with Simon in the schoolroom had been satisfactory, at least those under Lionel's watchful eye. He couldn't guess what she might do when night terrors struck his son. He could only hope she would not panic, as servants did, or repel Simon, as his mother had.

But Lionel had not been forthcoming with Sophie, and he regretted it. He would have to tell her before bedtime.

Bedtime, and Sophie. He savagely suppressed the thought.

Outside, Carter, his estate agent, rode up, in good time for their rounds. He dismounted and helped Sophie down.

Against a blustering wind, she pinned her skirts to her thighs and her straw bonnet to her head. Lionel savored the sight, his first opportunity to study her attractions unawares. She was still a buxom, healthy country lass, with rich chestnut hair and intelligent green eyes. Her creamy skin and rosy cheeks belied her age. He could hardly believe it had been almost twenty years since their glorious summer. She looked that much younger than he felt himself to be.

She and Carter shared a word, a smile, and then a laugh.

An ungovernable jealousy ripped him. He'd turned his back on Sophie a lifetime ago, he reminded himself, submitting to his father's rule, his father's fury. Sophie could talk, smile, and have a laugh with any man she chose. Absently fingering his neglected snuffbox, he summoned indifference. Sophie and Carter must have known each other for years to be on such easy terms. They made a handsome couple. For all he knew, outsider that he was, they could be a match.

He ground his teeth, vexed with the scene, but more vexed that he cared.

Sophie and Carter. Fine. It was none of Lionel's affair. She was here for his sons, and devil take the rest. He was master of his thoughts, his world. He opened a ledger, but his eyes swam over Tims's immaculate corrections.

Sophie was on his mind, under his skin, in his blood.

He'd left it to Mrs. Plumridge to settle his son's new tutor into an appropriate room. One far away, the tutor's room upstairs, would be safest from him, but one near the boys' rooms would be convenient for her whenever Simon's terrors struck. Even so, the chambermaid who slept within could fetch her from anywhere in the house.

Second thoughts assailed him. Simon's jeopardy aside, what had he been thinking to command Sophie to move in? In providing for very urgent needs of his three sons at home, he'd overlooked his own.

Because now Sophie would be at Wraxham House, not merely in the daytime, but at night, in a bed, under his very roof, stripping out of her dress at day's end and snuggling in under the covers, her night rail draping her generous bosom and—he imagined—her shapely legs. She would scissor them beneath the linen sheets, stretching one leg down, drawing up the other, and where they joined, the curls would be soft and brown, inviting to his touch, his tongue, his taste . . . Blast his ungovernable fantasies all to hell.

The lad who'd loved her would have been in paradise.

The man who wanted her—*admit it, soldier, you still want her*—was in hell.

Sophie, he knew, was headed for the schoolroom.

He shrugged into his riding coat and picked up his gloves to go meet Carter.

He wanted Sophie in his bed.

Which would never do. Only a month ago, he'd vowed to reform his decadent life. He wouldn't compromise her a second time. There was only one honorable way to get her in his bed.

Marriage.

But he couldn't marry her.

It wasn't that Sophie Bowerbank was penniless, or indeed, through her father, actually in debt to him. He didn't need a moneyed wife. Of late, he had an unexpected confidence that several years of honest work and simple frugal management would restore Wraxham to its former glory.

But he wouldn't marry her, not with a year's mourning still to honor and his three sons at home in disarray. The other three, as best he knew, were soldiering on in their expensive institutions. Like Lionel, Graeme, his heir, had a poetical, scholarly bent, and had eagerly left home for the university. From reports, James and Marcus were doing Lionel proud at Abercairn near the Wraxham properties in Scotland.

He reminded himself of his most compelling reason not to marry. He'd resolved to devote himself to those sons.

He squared his shoulders. Let the reform of his rakish, wastrel ways start here. He had estate rounds ahead of him, work to do, decisions to make. It irked him that he'd missed speaking to Sophie before heading out, but it relieved him to be able to leave his younger sons in such capable hands.

Sophia's hands. They obsessed him. She obsessed him. Every fiber of his being remembered her earnest touch. At the kissing gate, her hands had sought the small of his back and the nape of his neck, as she used to do those many years ago. He wanted to feel her again, skin to skin, limb to limb, muscle, tendon, sinew.

He strode across the greensward to the stables, away from her, cursing ripe oaths of self-condemnation.

He would master this. He'd lived with his shrew of a viscountess almost twenty years and managed never to shout at her or strike her. He could manage anything, even a decades-old obsession come back to taunt him.

At dusk, Lionel trudged up the private passage to his quarters, knee aching from a long day in a carriage. Better that than riding, which made it even worse. Near the top of the stairs, women were arguing, when he expected neither women nor contention here. Could it be Sophie? Turning spy in his own home, he held his breath and looked and listened.

"I understand that, madam, but Miss Bowerbank specifically

asked for the tutor's room beside the schoolroom." The formidable Mrs. Plumridge was holding forth, her breadth blocking any view of her target. He could see trunks, though, piled high as Penelope had ever piled hers on visits to friends' country houses.

"How very odd, as it has no room adjoining," the other woman argued, but he didn't recognize her breathy, cultured voice and couldn't see her form.

"Yes, madam, just the schoolroom," Mrs. Plumridge said.

"Miss Bowerbank mentioned nothing of the sort to me, and yet I'm sure she wanted us to have adjoining rooms."

Mrs. Plumridge huffed. "That is usual with companions."

A companion. Lionel almost cheered in appreciation. Clever woman, that Sophie. An old crone of a companion would quiet the gossips and scotch any designs he might have upon her person in the bargain. He couldn't think who Sophie might have found on such short notice.

Whoever the woman was, the redoubtable Mrs. Plumridge wasn't impressed. "I haven't the power to alter His Lordship's orders, madam. . . ."

Then his housekeeper stepped around the piles of luggage, revealing a glittering blond . . . beauty.

Lionel's jaw dropped. Sophie's companion was no old crone. She was small, slender, elegant, as richly dressed as any London lass, and evidently gently bred.

"But, my good Mrs. Plumridge," the woman persisted, her tone obliging, yet somehow strong as steel. "I cannot imagine His Lordship would want us treated as anything less than his guests for a country weekend. As I understand it, Miss Bowerbank will be tutoring Lord Wraxham's sons as a favor. If you would only send for her—"

"No need, Mrs. Plumridge." Lionel spoke up from the shadows on the stairs.

Mrs. Plumridge started, and the blonde covered a shriek with a dainty hand.

He continued, as courtesy demanded, "I'm sure we can

come to some satisfactory arrangement, Miss . . . ?"

Sophie's friend curtsied gracefully and offered him her be-ringed hand. "Celia Upton, my lord. It has been many years."

So many he did not remember them, or her, exactly. But he took the elegant hand, and executed his most polished bow. "Ah, Squire Upton's daughter."

She dimpled. "Yes, and if it please you, sir, Miss Bower-bank's companion."

"Most welcome," he said politely. "Now, what seems to be the matter?"

"There must be some confusion about our rooms. Sophie has been sent to the servants' quarters, hardly appropriate—"

"You and Miss Upton must have rooms on the family's floor. I wouldn't dream of relegating the reverend's and the squire's daughters to the servants' quarters. We have abundant rooms along the main hallway, including the boys' rooms at the opposite end."

"But, my lord—" Mrs. Plumridge objected.

"As I say, Mrs. Plumridge," he said curtly. He'd gone public with his offer. It was too late now.

Excusing himself, he bolted for his suite, barely taking proper leave. What had made him offer that?

A maudlin fit of sentimentality, that's what.

He'd meant for Sophie to live upstairs, at the opposite ends of his eighty-seven-roomed estate.

And he didn't want the beautiful Miss Celia Upton—whom he remembered now—anywhere near whatever was going to transpire between him and the woman he'd once loved heart and soul.

Chapter Six

About your Neck I could have flung my Arms,
And been all over Love, all over Charms;
Grasp and hang on your K—, and there have dy'd,
There breath[e] my gasping Soul out tho' deny'd.
    —The Fifteen Pleasures of a Virgin (1709)

Sophie shivered miserably. Her dress was still damp, her hair still dripping, and her temper in a twist. She couldn't look more ridiculous standing outside the imposing mahogany doors of Wraxham's august dining room. Her first full day of overseeing the Honorable Masters Westfall's education had ended an abject failure by anybody's measure, but emphatically by her own high standards of competence.

A lanky footman stationed beneath a gilded sconce looked straight past her soggy predicament.

"Could you just please summon Mrs. Plumridge for me?" she asked, teeth chattering.

The young servant opened the doors and blurted, "Mrs. Plumridge, ma'am, a lady for ye, and she looks half drowned."

Sophie sank in embarrassment. It wouldn't do for Lionel to see his tutor in such a sorry state. She'd only come because she couldn't find her room, and she needed Mrs. Plumridge to show her where to go.

But it was Lionel whose gleaming boots clicked across the marble floors. "Sophie? Good God!" he burst out, taking in her sopping wet tresses, her drenched dress, and her muddy, shredded slippers at a glance. His gaze stuck in the region of her bosom, and she looked down.

Her nipples poked up beneath the clinging bodice of her plain gray dress.

Oh my. She hadn't expected anything like this. Intrigued by his fixation, she slowly covered herself with her cold blue hands.

"What the devil—you look—drenched—" he stammered.

But everyone was crowding in behind him, eyes popping at the rarity—the novelty—of a gentlewoman dripping in distress.

Plump Mrs. Plumridge clenched the cupboard keys, and her stocky French chef brandished serving tongs. Assorted maids and footmen still bore baskets of bread, tureens of soups, platters of meat, and chafing dishes of vegetables hot from the kitchen. The twins squirmed, and Simon peeked out from behind them, his chocolate eyes wide with curiosity. Even her friend Celia was all a-flutter in her richest crimson silks.

Lionel shucked off his stylish waistcoat of midnight superfine, draped it over her shoulders, and buttoned it up to her neck.

Welcome warmth enveloped her, his warmth, remembered from that summer, and lately from the kissing gate. She breathed in the clean aroma of soap and rum, and then his own rich scent drifted up. She squeezed her eyes shut, savoring him, so near, so unexpectedly protective of her.

"Thank you, my lord," she managed, teeth chattering still.

But he was cursing under his breath, turning her from the idle scrutiny of the amused and curious. "I'll get to the bottom

58

of this, you scoundrels," he called back over his shoulder.

He meant Max and Alex.

"It wasn't their fault, my lord."

"On the contrary," he said grimly, "your condition bears the mark of one of their more inspired tutorial initiations."

He marched her away from them, his hands gentle but his voice grim. "What was it this time, an unexpected tumble into our front fountain? Or a balloon of sheep's gut filled with water and dropped on you from the parapets?"

"It was nothing of the sort, my lord." She pressed her lips together. He was so indignant. But it wouldn't do to laugh at her rescuer or his sons. Besides, she was coming to quite like his rapscallions. She wouldn't let them take the blame for her own clumsiness, even if it was ever so slightly possible that they'd known the rickety weir might not support a grown and not insubstantial woman when she leaned out to free their fishing line from an inconvenient willow branch.

He gave a skeptic's scowl. "So you say on two days' acquaintance." Slowing their pace, he turned her round an unfamiliar corner into terra incognita: a high, wide hallway adorned with riches. Where exactly was he taking her?

"They'd been such good boys all day long."

"Rubbish," he snorted. "They excel at that particularly ingenious diversion. Seduces one into thinking they have learned to mind."

"They asked if they might go fishing, down at the millpond."

Their millpond, where she and Lionel used to meet to read and kiss and talk and kiss and dream. Despite the many changes time had wrought in both of them, the pond had been the same, clear and pure and languid.

But he didn't even acknowledge he recalled their times there, and she forged down the unfamiliar hallway, wondering how something she remembered graphically could have no significance for him. He couldn't have forgotten. Not where she was so acutely aware of every physical, sensual thing about him, the familiar and the changed. He seemed taller, broader in the shoulders, more urbane in his address, more manly and desirable.

Blast! It was as she feared. After only moments in his presence, she was engrossed with him. Whereas he—he was living up to his vow of self-control, concerned only to show his tutor to her room, thus dispensing with her for the night.

Which might help her preserve her reputation.

But not help her realize her dreams and fantasies.

She hid her frustration behind a heartfelt scold. "It wasn't as though you'd bothered to explain their rules to me, and you were nowhere to be found. I couldn't well let them go off alone."

"Responsible of you to take that tack, if ineffective. At day's end, they're like furloughed sailors after months at sea."

"You might have warned me of that too, my lord."

"I might have done, if you had not been late arriving, and I, saddled with appointments for the day."

Which didn't make it her fault, she thought, but her indignation slid into uneasiness. Lionel was picking up their pace, leading her deeper into heaven knew where. Mrs. Plumridge must have taken her to her new quarters in the tutor's room by a different route. Posh Turkish carpets Sophie had not yet walked on muffled Lionel's footsteps, and hers, and she was lost in the luxurious vastness of Wraxham House.

In moments, they entered a high, wide hallway, its windows on the south side open to the fresh April air. To the north, doors stood at military intervals along walls lit lavishly with tapers. Great oil portraits of aristocratic ancestors hung atop antique tapestries that stretched from the ceiling to the floor. Along the walls between massive carved doors, ornate French chairs invited one to pause and sit awhile. Marble-topped tables awaited books or gloves, while priceless Chinese vases as tall as her waist stood merely to be admired.

"This isn't the way to the tutor's room," she said, letting go of Lionel's forearm in confusion.

"Indeed. I ordered your trunk moved to a room I use for guests," he said blandly.

"Whatever for, my lord?"

"Don't be coy, Sophie," he said in that cool urbane tone she was fast coming to dislike. "Your companion persuaded me that nothing less would suit two such gentlewomen as yourselves. You cannot say you had no hand in it."

Blast Celia. Sophie hadn't had a hand in it. But to say so would make her friend look bad. "This is the family's quarters, my lord."

"For family and guests, yes."

"A tutor is an employee and should be housed separately."

"On the contrary, some would say a tutor is more a part of the family than any other of the staff. I agree. The boys are at the east end of the hall. My suite is at the west end, opposite. Yours and Miss Upton's rooms"—he stopped near his end of the long, long gallery—"are here."

Oh my. "Here" was much too close. "This cannot be wise, my lord, given our . . ."

"Our history?" he finished for her soberly.

She looked down at her ruined shoes, instantly thrust back to their long-ago intimacy. She'd tried to shrug it off. But with the slightest provocation from the old earl's bawdy books, her obsession with Lionel, her dream of passion with him, had roared back into her life with an appalling vengeance. Against all reason, all experience, Lionel Westfall, the man, still drew her to him.

While his feelings, if any, were well under his control.

"What's the matter, Sophie? Afraid that I will ravish you if our bedchambers are too close?"

No, I am afraid that you will not, she thought.

But she said, "No, my lord, of course not."

"Anyone can see that you would be much safer from my designs a way up in the tutor's room," he said with an ironic glint in his gray eyes. "No lord ever ravished lady there."

She bridled at his taunt. She didn't need to be reminded

that a man of his lofty status could have any woman anywhere. Or not, if he chose not to.

"I quite see your point, my lord."

He turned her to face him, his gray eyes brooding in the soft candlelight. "*Lionel*, damn it. Say *Lionel*, Sophie. We were friends once."

"We were more than friends, my lord," she said, determined to face the truth and make him face it too.

His shadowed jaw clenched in self-reproach. "True, and I am sorry for it. Sorry for any pain I may have caused you. For any dreams I may have dashed."

"You were far too young," she said.

"No," he said harshly. "You were far too young. I was a spineless guttersnipe."

She smiled weakly. "You could not have had a more willing conspirator." She was the one who'd gone running to him. Who'd met him with open heart and eager arms.

"Good God, Sophie, you were a child," he said starkly, "if a child in a woman's body. If it's any comfort, I went on to live an absurdly frivolous life."

"If you did, my lord, I could not take comfort in it."

A certain vindication, but not comfort.

"The estate deserves a better man, and my sons a better father."

She did not want him to be better. She wanted him to be her lover. But she said blandly, "An admirable ambition, my lord."

"I've taken a vow of reform, and you are witness to it," he continued. And a note of genuine earnestness slipped through his urbanity, a remnant of the boy she'd loved inside the man she couldn't help wanting. "You have nothing to fear from me," he added.

Nothing to hope rather, she thought, frustration knotting her senses. Here she had been indulging bawdy fantasies, and the man who'd introduced her to sensuality was indulging himself in prudish notions of reform.

"I'm not afraid of you," she said.

"Damn it, you never were, and that was the problem."

"You left me sweet memories, my lord."

"I left you. I see that now, and I swear I'll make it up to you."

"There's nothing to make up, my lord."

"On the contrary. I will help you with your father. Protect you from my sons. Protect you from myself. It is the very least that I can do."

The very least? She tightened his waistcoat around her, feeling a deeper chill than from the cold spring water in the pond. He wasn't just guilty for what he'd done. He must feel guilty for what he no longer felt. How foolish her scandalously bawdy, life-affirming fantasies about this man had been. How very vain.

He tipped her chin, his fingers branding her.

She could only meet his kind gray gaze.

"I will not accost you again, Miss Sophie Bowerbank, friend of my youth," said the earnest Lionel, whom she had loved. "Our friendship was the only time of my life that was not misspent. I want you to feel safe here. Will you trust me to redeem myself?"

How ironic. After her lifetime of chastity, he sought redemption while she leaned toward sin.

She managed a small smile. "I will try to trust you, my lord."

His hard visage softened with relief. "We need you here, my sons and I."

"Yes, my lord."

"*Lionel*," he insisted.

"Lionel," she whispered. *My friend.*

"Better," he said softly. And gently touched her cheek with a knuckle, an oddly intimate but—she understood this now—a merely friendly gesture. "I am sorry my twins were such a trial today. They are good boys at heart, but spoiled and bored. I am counting on you to help me turn them around. Help them love the country as I once did."

With the briefest smile and a promise to send up a hot bath

and supper, he opened the door for her to enter her splendid, solitary chamber.

Hours later, clean and warm and full, Sophie snuggled in a chair with a branch of candles and a geography book, preparing tomorrow's lesson. Or rather trying.

She had washed away the scent of Lionel, but not the image, not the sense. And not her disappointment. Face it, she had accepted his offer to move in for all the wrong reasons: for one wrong reason uppermost. She had wanted him to want her again. She had thought proximity might be enough to— oh, not win him back, she who had never had him, but give her another chance just to be with him. Body and soul, heart and mind.

No, she was grown beyond that naive girl. Tonight she had been ready to settle for body and body, his and hers, together again at last. She was weary of her virtue, burdened by her reputation, and bored to tears with innocence. She wanted a woman's knowledge. She wanted passion with a man. And everything about meeting up with Lionel again told her she could have all that with him.

But only if he wanted it with her.

Evidently with that wretched kiss, he had satisfied himself that she did not measure up to his London ladies, perhaps even, for all she knew, to his late wife. Perhaps she never had. Her heart churned with vexation. He regretted that they'd shared even that one passing kiss. He saw her as a friend. He spoke of family favors—his to her father, hers to his sons—as if he'd read her mind and disapproved of her wanton imaginings.

How old she must appear to him, how bookish and naive. How ordinary and unwomanly.

She gave herself a mental shake. She would have to be what he had hired her to be. Tutor to his sons. She flipped from map to map and forced herself to concentrate on the work at hand. How could she bring to life the capitals of the world?

Should she embark on a history of Athens? Paris? Rome? What would appeal to boys? Sabers and fast horses, no doubt. Blood and desert nights. Suspicion and betrayal.

What about . . . ah, the siege of Troy. She went to her trunk and rummaged for her books. While she'd been taking a dunking in the old millpond, her few dresses had been pressed and put away, but the books had not been touched. Not even the bawdy ones. The rest were her father's—and so her—treasures, these latest histories by Gibbon and Macauley. She looked around for where to put them. There were no shelves along the walls, just a wealth of dark old oils. Evidently *guests* did not come to country houses bearing books.

So where . . . ? Ah, there, beneath the tall sashed windows on the deep sill. She gathered up half a dozen volumes and hugged them to her breasts.

Tap, tap, tap, came a knocking on the door.

Startled, Sophie nearly dropped her books. Drat, it must be Celia. Sophie had too much to prepare for tomorrow's lessons to engage in a friendly tête-à-tête. But why would Celia be knocking at her hallway door? Surely she would knock at the inner door that connected their rooms.

It couldn't be Lionel. Sophie's heart thumped, and her mind raced. Could it? Could she have misread his painfully correct conduct when he deposited her here? Could there be an intimate, coded message behind his ordering her bath and meal sent to her room? Perhaps this was how lovers made secret rendezvous.

Tap, tap, tap. Oh, for heaven's sake. And wouldn't Celia have come right in?

Sophie ran nervous fingers over her prim night rail, its fraying country tatting hiding her wrists and concealing her throat. It was hardly a seductive garment. Still, she should put on her dressing gown lest she appear positively brazen, as women did in some of those sensual stories. She tucked the bawdy books behind the histories on the sill and hurried to her wardrobe.

Tap, tap, tap. Stars, she was not cut out for this. Dare she answer?

She must dare.

This was why she'd moved into Lionel's stately home. In spite of his protests to protect her from himself, she wasn't giving up yet. With a tremor of anticipation, she reached for her dressing gown, slid her arms into its practical woolen warmth, sashed it loosely, and smoothed her still damp hair. Heart pounding, she padded across the finest carpet she had ever trod upon, unlocked the latch, and cracked the inner door.

"Sophie, dearest!" a familiar voice breathed sweetly.

Sophie opened the door, heart sinking.

Celia swept in, resplendent in a crimson evening dress, her delicate blond beauty luminous under the quiet chamber lights.

Fool, Sophie admonished herself. Idle dreamer. Pathetic spinster.

"You did not use the door that joins our room," Sophie mustered.

"Oh, that. It seems it's locked. I'll order it unlocked in the morning. Meanwhile . . ." Celia lifted her hands to celebrate the high-ceilinged, spacious room and twirled on silken slippers. "Oh, Sophie, I could get used to this! Isn't it grand? Aubusson carpets and walls lined with silk. And look at that exquisite French commode."

The two-drawer, round-bellied little commode was gilded and ornately carved, but Sophie had been too consumed with the Lord of Wraxham's attributes to admire his furniture. "It's all rather staggeringly grand, Celie."

Undeterred, Celia homed in on a painting on the wall. A horsy scene, with foxhounds. "Oooh, and you have a Stubbs, commissioned, no doubt. How very sporting. This must usually be a man's room. Mine has a Vermeer, a lady in velvet. I cannot believe you worked here for three years and never told me."

"I worked in the library and belowstairs in the archives, and never came near the guest quarters. Though the collection is impressive in its own right," she added, and instantly regretted it. On principle, she never vied with her competitive friend for superiority in experience, knowledge, or possessions.

"But you came every day, and now we are ensconced here . . . in luxury. It suits me so much better than the grange, don't you think?" Celia said playfully, her spirits still high.

"I'm sure Wraxham House suits His Lordship's employees better than the lowly huts and cottages they came from," Sophie said, reminding her friend of her station and their purpose here.

"My accomplishments show to so much more advantage if I can play the earl's honored guest," Celia went on, quite full of herself. Then she pulled a long face and said, "Oh dear, I quite forgot. I haven't asked about your heroic skirmish with the pond."

Celia had a way of exaggerating almost anything.

"I'm afraid the pond got the better of me."

"But are you all right? As your companion, I was derelict in my duty. I should have come offering a towel, or at least commiseration. But His Lordship kept me after dinner over a wicked game of chess."

"Did he succumb?" Sophie asked. Celia played a cunning game of chess, and Sophie couldn't fathom which of them might be the keener player.

"Lord Wraxham, succumb?" Celia's lips curved in a self-satisfied smile. "La, no. I'm not so confident of my welcome to defeat our host on the first night of our stay."

Sophie had to admire such subtlety, but she didn't like to think that Lionel had been fooled. "I should have thought he would let a guest, and a lady, win."

Celia shrugged an alabaster shoulder. "He did seem quite diverted that a mere squire's daughter could put him on his mettle."

"No doubt," Sophie said, scolding herself that she had not

put him on his mettle. No, she had practically fallen at his feet, and he'd spent the evening enjoying another woman's charms. Celia would soon have him wrapped around her little finger.

Goose. Widget. Dunderhead.

"He must not know I had a season or two in London." Celia pouted prettily. "He seemed quite disturbed by your accident, by the by. Pray tell me he did not read you out for hazarding such danger."

Sophie glared at her very best friend. It was beyond bearing to stand here, plain and bookish in her drab woolen dressing gown, while Celia, a vaunted beauty, carried on in silks.

"He did not read me out for anything, Celie," Sophie said. She could share *nothing* that had passed between her and Lionel with her friend. She could, however, express her disapproval of their quarters. "He has been generous. He even overlooked your appalling forwardness in insisting on these rooms."

"How forward can I have been, Sophie, if he consented?"

"Perhaps so forward as to ruin any appearance of propriety."

Celia twinkled. "That is the great conundrum of propriety, dear Sophie. As I understand it, anyone can get away with anything in these great country houses, appearances be damned."

"Celia, that's a shocking notion," Sophie said. A shocking, and very interesting, notion. One that might well suit her plans, plans Celia mustn't have an inkling of. "What kind of companion did you purport to be?"

Celia took her hand. "Not to worry, my dear friend. We shall keep the door between our rooms unlocked as a barrier to any indiscretion. Moreover, by my being here, I serve as witness, don't you see? Did anything happen between you and Lord Wraxham tonight?"

"No, nothing." Sophie gulped, and her face heated. Blast! She was no good at subterfuge.

"No, of course not, you were alone together only a few

minutes," Celia went on, swelling with the importance of her role. "I think it's rather telling that he chose to play publicly with me, ensuring that no one could see any impropriety in the brief time he spent alone with you. And then, quite late, everyone went to bed."

How to stop Celia's blather? Sophie had lessons to prepare for tomorrow. She pointed Celia firmly to the door that joined their rooms and hinted broadly, "You must be tired. But we accomplished quite a bit for our first day, don't you think?"

"You see how nicely it will work out?" Celia went on, oblivious. "Your reputation will be—"

"Good night, Celia."

"—completely unexceptional, and we shall enjoy ourselves in opulence and—"

"Thank you, Celia, and good night."

At last, Celia floated through the doorway, and Sophie closed the door behind her. It was amusing to hear Celia chatter like a schoolgirl, to see her dazzled by the lord and luxuries of Wraxham.

But Sophie had assumed a companion would stay somehow in the background. Celia seemed bent on establishing herself smack in the middle of Sophie's mission.

Sophie slumped into the brocaded chair and took up the siege of Troy, but her concentration was in tatters. Helen, Achilles, Agamemnon—she drilled herself on their actions and alliances, committing passages from *The Iliad* to memory.

Gradually, fatigue overtook her, and she was drifting amidst images of caftans and desert ponies when *rap, rap,* an insistent knocking startled her awake.

Her book lay open on her lap. She closed it and stood, drowsy and annoyed by yet another interruption to her evening.

Rap, rap, it came louder and more insistent.

She hastened to give Celia a piece of her mind.

Chapter Seven

Thus thro' mistake I rashly plung'd my Life
Into that Gulph of Miseries a Wife.
With joyful Arms I thus embrac'd my Fate,
Believ'd too soon, was undeceiv'd too late.
                    —The Pleasures of a Single Life,
                    or, The Miseries of Matrimony (1701)

Lionel shoved his shirttails into his hastily clad breeches and
rapped on Sophie's chamber door, willing his actions to mask
the shakes. He hated surprising her with this, but hadn't found
the time to take her aside for the lengthy explanation she deserved about Simon's terrors. And his own.

Now Simon was far gone into one of his fits, and inconsolable. His screams, muffled by the chambermaid, cut to the
marrow of Lionel's bones.

Sophie had to know. He needed her help.

He knocked again, the same short rap, the same military
precision. On leaving his London life behind, he'd fallen back
on his old air of command. He expected order, needed it, and

hated it. The world had hailed him as a hero for taking that critical hill in the thick of battle and dark of night, but he knew the bitter truth. He'd sent his men on a desperate charge, ill advised by his superiors and ill prepared by himself. He'd gained a furlough of disputed ground and lost half his troops.

God, he hated nighttime, the unknown, and screams.

He pulled on his coat, still damp from his rescue of Sophie in the dining room.

Rap. Rap.

Sophie, wake up.

Fingers fumbled at the iron latch, the door cracked open, and a sultry, sleep-thickened voice murmured, "For heaven's sake, Celie. It's the middle of the night."

"It's not Miss Upton, Sophie, and I'd prefer that she not know."

"My lord?" Sophie croaked, and the gap creaked closed. He heard rustling in the dark. She was putting on her dressing gown, which made him think of how she'd looked in that wet dress. Bugger all. He was a cad to think of her like that when he was dragging her from her bed to see Simon at his worst. Himself at his worst.

She cracked the door again.

"Come," he ordered, through the narrow band into her dark room. In the hall his hastily lit candle shed a faint light. "Simon needs you."

"Needs me? How?" she asked, her voice clearing. She stepped into the hall, frowning in confusion, her warm brown hair tumbling about her shoulders, kissing the hidden mounds of her generous breasts.

"This way," he said. Resolutely quashing his attraction to her, he tucked her hand in the crook of his arm and led her down the quiet, dark hall. She was tall, and matched him stride for aching stride. His knee was always worse after an active day.

"At night, my son has fits, like nightmares, only worse. Not every night, and they pass, and he remembers nothing after.

He hasn't had one in a week, and I'd— It was too much to hope they were tapering off."

"Simon has fits," she repeated. Anger edged her voice. "You should have told me that before I agreed to this position."

He glanced down. "Would you have accepted it, regardless?"

She gave a husky snort—a negative? He couldn't tell—but her step beside him did not falter. "Perhaps you could tell me now. Fits?"

"He wakes up, startled, eyes wide open, except that he isn't awake. He often screams, terrified of . . . spiders, sometimes. Sometimes snakes. And apparently from things he utters lately, a monster is trying to kill his mother."

"Who is dead."

"Yes."

"And this lasts the night?"

"Usually not, just half an hour, an hour. After his mother's death, his fits became both longer and more frequent."

"What do you do for them?"

"After I fired his former nurse, a frivolous young woman, I sought out a new doctor, a new nurse, and a new regimen. Nurse Nesbit was instructed to follow it to the letter. Unfortunately she is visiting ailing parents, which leaves Simon in the hands of some inexperienced—"

"*I* am inexperienced, my lord," Sophie said, a hitch of anxiety in her voice.

"Ah, but you are caring and concerned, and have a way with boys."

She said no more, and they arrived at Simon's door, his screams muffled but plain to hear.

Sophie's hand tightened on his elbow. "What must I do?"

He let out a breath of exasperation. *Make things right.* Would to God somebody could. "For the moment, watch. Perhaps you'll learn something that will guide you in your dealings with him. And, Sophie . . ." He waited until she looked at him. "He won't know it's you. He doesn't know it's me."

A bloodcurdling scream looped out into the gallery, a woman's voice scolding, and footsteps, heavy and light, running.

"Good God. He's loose," Lionel blurted and burst through the door to save his son.

"Oh, for pity's sake!" Sophie cried, and followed Lionel in.

The rational, classically educated part of Sophie's mind knew that a person's heart could not be in her throat. But when she heard Simon's soul-shattering scream, hers was.

A dozen tapers lit the room to fend off demons in the night. Pale, timid little Simon screamed and thrashed about as if the very hounds of hell were tearing him limb from limb.

A hefty chambermaid, red-faced from chasing him, held him at arm's length.

Sophie's heart cracked. The woman shouldn't touch the poor distraught child, let alone spend another night with him.

"I can't get him in the cold bath, my lord," the maid complained.

"For God's sake, woman, you're three times his size."

She gasped with the effort of constraining the boy. "The little demon tried to rip my arms off." She shook the torn sleeves of her simple shift at him.

Lionel glared down at her. "He's only seven."

"If you think I'll spend another night with him, my lord, you are as mad as he is."

Simon couldn't be mad. In the schoolroom, he was the dearest, gentlest child. Just this afternoon Sophie had read to him Mrs. Smith's poem on a hedgehog from one of her little books for children. His great brown eyes had been bright with interest.

"You may return to London in the morning, Mrs. Seagraves," Lionel ordered, drawing on some deep reserve of restraint and command Sophie had never seen in him. "With your full pay and a reference. You are not to talk about my son's condition. If I find that you have, you will never work again."

The woman stomped out, making the toys on a high shelf

rattle. Lionel sank to his knees and grasped Simon's thrashing, skinny arms in his large man's hands.

Sophie couldn't bear it. She sat down beside them and reached for Simon. "Let me take him, my lord."

"You could be seriously hurt," Lionel said hoarsely.

"I'm not afraid. He's very small," Sophie said.

"He's not in his right mind, Sophie. He may not be a demon, but he has the strength of one."

Sophie shook her head in disgust. "Hand me your son, my lord. If I am to tutor him, I should handle this. My way."

The oddest expression crossed Lionel's face, a mix of astonishment and gratitude. He released his struggling son.

"We'll try that cold bath in a moment," Lionel said.

"Not a cold bath, my lord," Sophie said, horrified. "I was just dowsed myself. I can hardly think of anything more distressing than to be plunged into icy water. Unnnf," she grunted as Simon freed a leg and kicked her in the shin.

Lionel winced. "His surgeon orders it, to break the spell."

"Surely not Dr. Maitland," she said. Wraxham's war-hardened young physician would yank a tooth out in a minute, but to relieve pain, not inflict it.

"No. His London surgeon," Lionel said.

"There must be a better way, my lord."

"His doctor warned that changing regimens could set him back."

"Ah, then," she said acidly, "you must believe that the present regimen is an improving one."

Lionel blew out a breath of exasperation. "Very well, Miss Bowerbank. What exactly do you recommend?"

"For this dear child, something less draconian, my lord," Sophie said, her voice husky with compassion.

Lionel. When he heard her tone, he wanted her to call him *Lionel,* reform and promises be damned. He wanted to erase the years and rank that separated them and be friends. But he needed her to understand how to help his son.

The boy was heedless of her touch, but she smoothed his

hair tenderly. "What could his doctor have been thinking?"

"I saw only the best," he said, defending himself.

"You met the man yourself then."

"Yes."

"And . . . ?"

"He didn't think my son was mad. He advocated less draconian treatments than Simon's previous doctor had promoted. And he assured me of his past success."

But now that Sophie challenged Lionel about it, he remembered Sir Roger Fotherington. His office in Mayfair had been more notable for its social amenities than its medical accoutrements. The man had exuded a certain blasé competence, aimed to put him on an equal footing with cantankerous quality.

Like himself.

Like his bloody privileged, arrogant, decadent self.

And so of course, seeking an expedient solution to Simon's misery, Lionel had listened.

"And that regimen was . . . ?" Sophie prodded. Simon bucked beneath her hands, but she hugged him closer to her bosom.

"The doctor recommended several things: the simplest course of study to keep Simon's thoughts from becoming overwrought. A bland diet so as not to precipitate a fit from digestive upset. Nothing to eat or drink before he goes to bed. In his room windows nailed shut, toys put away at night, nothing left out with which he might harm himself. Strong nurses to pin him to his bed and keep him from harming himself. And then when all else fails, as it has tonight, cold baths to jolt him from his spasms."

Sophie snorted softly. "That sounds like treatment for a bedlamite, my lord. How *could* you accept it?"

"It seemed more reasoned than the gags, shackles, and locked closets ordered by the doctors his mother retained," Lionel said, forgetting his rule never to disparage the mother of his sons. He had discovered Penelope's regimen only after her death, to his eternal regret.

Because he'd let her have her way. He'd renounced his natural authority over his sons and allowed her full power over them. Over his most vulnerable son. The son whose terrors brought up shameful, unmanly terrors of his own.

His abysmal failure as a father slammed him in the face. It was no comfort that he'd banished both that doctor and the impressionable and not always responsible French nurse.

"I am neither a doctor nor a parent," Sophie went on reasonably, "but I can hardly imagine a course of treatment more cruel and less likely to soothe a seven-year-old in the throes of an attack."

Put that way, neither could he. But his pent-up frustration over his son's continued sufferings poured out in cutting irony. "No doubt your regimen guarantees improvement, Miss Bowerbank."

She winced at his harshness but lifted her chin over Simon's head. "I am not a doctor. I have no regimen to offer."

"Then what?"

"It's just that . . . if he were my son . . ." She grunted with the effort to contain another spasm.

"Which he isn't, but go on. . . ."

"And I his mother, I would simply hold and comfort him just as I am doing now."

Lionel frowned. "None of the doctors suggested that."

"You can't possibly mean that no one ever tried simple comfort and reassurance."

"They tried that at first. Must have done," he said, but he didn't know. Penelope, older than he by seven years, and more cunning by seventy, had subtly and effectively undermined his efforts to be a father to his sons. He'd escaped her manipulations and his own memories of war to the distractions of gaming halls, sporting venues, and other women.

Lionel closed his eyes and muttered, "He worsened after his mother's death. He's worsening now."

Simon's legs pumped wildly against his tutor, as if he were fleeing the monsters in his dream. Like Lionel's men running up the hill.

"No baths," Sophie whispered. Then she wrapped her arms around Simon, her eyes bright with a compassion Lionel had never seen in Simon's nurses, and softly crooned an ancient lullaby.

Simon didn't seem to hear. Anguish distorted his face, as real and horrible as the ravaged faces Lionel had seen on men at war. He should be holding his son himself, fighting the terrors with his man's strength, if only he could bear it. There was something shameful to his standing by uselessly as Sophie's best effort brought no change.

Minutes ticked by, a quarter hour, and neither Simon's fearful moans nor frantic spasms abated. He kicked and thrashed against her body, hurting her, to judge by her grunts. But her hand found the crown of his head, and her fingers drew small circles in his scalp.

Lionel's deadened heart shifted in his chest. His youngest, most needy child was draped in the arms of the woman he should have married, inconsolable and yet consoled. In these last years of Simon's terrors, Lionel had never once seen Penelope hold her youngest son to her bosom, waking, sleeping, or in his terrors.

Gradually Simon quieted and dozed, a testament to Sophie's patient sacrifice. The clock chimed the half hour after midnight, and a short time later, Simon woke, trembling and confused. "Is Mama home yet, Papa?"

"Mama won't be coming home, son."

"Why are we in London, Papa?"

"We're not. We're at home at Wraxham House."

"Oh," he said, a frown wrinkling his pale brow. "Hate snakes."

Then he nestled his head under Sophie's chin and drifted back to sleep.

* * *

Sophie insisted on staying with Simon through the night, but Lionel ordered her to bed.

"He's done for one evening. I will get someone to watch him."

"Not that horrid substitute."

"No, not her. Another one, Sophie, someone easily wakened who would come and fetch me, which she will not have to do."

Then he said, "You still love debate."

They had debated David Hume and Adam Smith in between hot kisses. Amidst the guttering candles, he thought he detected a blush.

But she stiffened and said crossly, "No, I'm just trying to do my job, ill though you have defined it, my lord."

Lionel, he thought stubbornly. They had been friends once, and her friendship now would be his only relief from the new burden of the earldom and new demands of fatherhood.

"You'll do it better on a good night's sleep," he said, stopping at her door.

Her shoulders slumped. "I thought common sense would win the day. I'm disappointed that my efforts didn't help."

He reached for her hand and squeezed it. "They didn't hurt. His doctor warns there may be no change for years. He's seen it go away."

"I don't know what to do."

He knew what he wanted her to do, but it was carnal, low, and on a bed and without clothes, and he had promised not to harm her.

So he said, "Care for us, Sophie. Care for us all."

She gave him a tired, rueful smile.

He thought it was beautiful.

She glanced back at Simon. "It seems that I do care, my lord."

She cared for his son. After his shameful showing, she couldn't possibly care for him.

Chapter Eight

And first, the greatest lasting'st Plague of Life,
Husband; the Constant Jaylor of a wife,
A proud insulting domineering thing,
Abroad a subject, but at Home a King,
There he in State does Arbitrary Reign,
And lordlike pow'r do's o'er his wife maintain.
——The Maid's Vindication, Or, the Fifteen
Comforts of Living a Single Life (1707)

Sophie couldn't think when she'd ever seen two such hangdog hobbledehoys as the Honorable Masters Max and Alex Westfall. They presented themselves at her desk in her schoolroom the next morning, scrubbed and polished and on time.

"Good morning, Miss Bowerbank," they said, as she had taught them.

"Good morning, Max and Alex. I trust you got a good night's sleep and are ready for the siege of Troy."

They looked down at their gleaming shoes. Simon stood behind them, a little pale from his taxing night. But his chocolate eyes were bright with worry over his brothers' predicament.

Max swallowed nervously. "Yes, ma'am, we are. Ready for Troy, that is. But Father says that first we must apologize for yesterday."

Sophie drew a complete and utter blank. Surely they didn't think—Lionel didn't think—they had anything to do with Simon's dreadful evening. It had been awful enough without blaming them.

"Not that we actually *did* anything," Alex added in the gaping silence.

"It's what we didn't do," Max explained.

Sophie waited, uncertain what he meant.

"You're the one who said that it would hold her," Alex said.

Max glowered. "You're the one who bet it wouldn't."

Then it dawned on her what they were trying to say. "You mean about the pond."

"Yes, Miss Bowerbank. The weir," Max said gravely. "It held us when we tried it, even if it was a little wobbly."

"But Papa said we should have known it might not be strong enough for you."

"Not that you're too big or anything, like Mrs. Plumridge."

"Or that new French chef would be."

"Monsieur Laframboise," Max said, his French accent quite good.

"No, it wouldn't have held either of them," said Alex.

"Probably not," Max agreed.

Alex clasped his hands together gravely. "Papa said we should have warned you."

Max darted him a censuring look. "And you should not have laughed."

"I did not," Alex huffed, ". . . at first."

"You shouldn't have laughed at all, Papa said. Even if it was funny," Max added, then winced at his blunder. "He didn't laugh *much*, Miss Bowerbank, honest, and I tried not to."

Simon's eyes widened with concern.

"Gentlemen," Sophie interrupted, an unaccustomed warmth stealing over her. Lionel had defended her. "Are you offering an apology?"

"Yes, ma'am."

"We are."

Sophie waited until the twins were each looking directly at her, condemned men before the gibbet. "Then I accept."

They let out a joint whoosh of relief. Then Max said, "We're forgiven?"

"Ummm," Sophie said, to temporize. "I could have been hurt. Or drowned."

"We would have saved you, Miss Bowerbank," Alex, who'd perpetrated the bet and initiated the laugh, assured her. "We know how to swim, and we are exceedingly brave."

"But what if you hadn't been strong enough to save me, you in your wet, heavy clothes and me in mine?"

Their gazes slid sideways.

"Didn't occur to us," Max mumbled.

"If you had warned me, you could have saved me discomfort and embarrassment. You wouldn't want anyone to do that to you. Especially a guest in your father's home. It wasn't worthy of you, or honorable, you know. Your father will take that into account before you have any guests of your own."

"I don't always think. I will do better. I can do better," Alex volunteered.

"Papa says we must learn not to be impetuous," Max added.

"Yes, and do you know what *impetuous* means?"

"No, ma'am," they said in uneasy unison.

"It means that you did something in haste, on the spur of the moment, without thinking of the consequences. Or in the matter of my danger on the wobbly weir, it means that you *didn't* do something, even though the consequences of not doing it could have been bad."

They blinked, and she imagined the concept was new to them. Yet it seemed to register. She put them to their illustrated history of the Trojan War, and turned anxiously to work with

81

Simon on his simple sums. Except for his pallor, he seemed unaffected by last night's ordeal. He finished his tasks so quickly that she couldn't resist putting a more difficult lesson before him despite the limits Lionel had set.

Simon had just started reading one of Mrs. Trimmer's tracts for children when Sophie felt a prickle down her spine.

She was being watched.

Lionel stood in the doorway, in country tweeds and polished riding boots, lordly and imposing and delicious. Her stomach dipped with that intoxicating desire remembered from their secret meetings and known only too well from her recent fantasies. Amazing that a man like him had ever given her the slightest notice.

He gestured to the door, and stepped back outside. She patted Simon on the shoulder, said a word to Max and Alex, and slipped out to join him, anticipation pulsing through her.

Up close, he was freshly shaved. His face had a healthy youthfulness, except for the haunting scar that cut a white path across one tawny brow. She wanted to feel the smooth, flat plane of his jaw beneath her fingertips. She wanted to test the texture of his lips.

"They apologized properly then," he said flatly.

Her fantasy evaporated, she was vexed by her imagination and his control. "Almost prettily, my lord. They must have had some practice."

He let out a puff of paternal exasperation. "Bloody little rapscallions."

"If memory does not deceive me, you and your brothers were once much the same," she said lightly.

But he was not amused. "We were lectured and soundly disciplined. I trust you were as strict with my sons."

His dark tone pricked her. "I stopped short of birching them, if you don't mind, my lord."

"I will save that for the next time," he said grimly.

"My lord, what an appalling thing to say. Surely you wouldn't beat them. They just have high spirits."

He snorted, but did not back down.

"It's Simon who concerns me," she went on.

He folded his arms across his chest and frowned. "He seemed fine just now."

"All may not be what it seems. He is advanced rather far beyond the course of study his last tutor set for him."

Lionel shook his head. "That is exactly what his doctor recommended: simpler mental endeavors that will not overexcite his mind."

"I beg your pardon, my lord. But that sounds like feeding straw instead of oats to your best carriage horse to calm him down. The horse would starve."

He blew out a breath, a stab at patience. "There has to be a balance, Sophie, between nothing, something, and too much. Too much in the daytime, and his nighttime episodes will worsen. We're aiming for peace of mind."

"For him or for you?" she said, exasperated.

He looked as if she'd punched him in the face. "For him, of course. Sophie, I am giving him the best doctors, the best nurses."

"Spoken like a man who only sees his son an hour a day, my lord."

"An hour a day for the last seven years of his life," Lionel corrected her. "I see what you're saying, and you're right. I haven't spent enough time with him. You, however, have barely spent a week."

"Even so, my lord, he's such a very bright boy, and he seems bored," she persisted. "I recommend stepping up his studies."

"It goes against every recommendation," he said with a heavy sigh.

But he did not say no.

"If I add a bit of history and geography, he can study with the twins for a portion of the day. He thinks his older brothers are all the crack."

Lionel's hand reached in his jacket and brought out his ever-present snuffbox, an emblem of the urbane, unreachable lord he was. It put her off. Perhaps he meant it to put her off.

"If we try and fail, we can go back to a simpler course."

His fist tightened around the gold-enameled box. "If you are wrong, Sophie, you may face some long, difficult nights with Simon."

She'd won. She gave him a solemn nod. "I am up to that, if I am wrong."

"I must do the assizes this afternoon. If you would kindly keep the twins under your care, I would prefer not to see them in my court this afternoon."

He stalked off, leaving her standing, musing about the man he had become. That summer, they'd never had a falling out. She'd never seen him angry, and she had loved him then.

So what had she won if she'd just driven him away?

And why did she find this taller, broader, brooding man, with his mix of strong emotions and everything held back, more compelling than the gentle, poetical lad?

In the schoolroom a few days later, Sophie twirled her father's prized globe, its leather surface smooth beneath her fingers. She had borrowed it to illustrate the farmost boundaries of the ancient Grecian world, naturally not shown on the schoolroom's modern model. She'd taken the boys deep into the fall of Troy. Max, Alex, even Simon studied the ancient borders, and returned to their scale model of the siege of Troy and its Trojan horse, determined to make it look just right.

The siege would take place tomorrow, and they planned to invite their father. They were doing so well. She was doing well with them. As far as she knew, the twins hadn't drummed up any more trouble. And Simon was sleeping through the night.

She'd been right. The smart little tyke had just been bored. She'd included him in the other boys' lessons, taught him backgammon and chess, and read with him each night at bedtime. He was brighter, happier, and his terrors had not returned.

He bent his chestnut head over his clay model of the hollow-bellied horse, intent and competent. The twins had appropriated a table from the kitchens belowstairs, mud from the gardens, and straw from the stables to build a model walled city for Simon's horse to enter and its soldiers to defeat.

In the forenoon she watched for a moment by the schoolroom's tall, mullioned windows. It was early May, and two stylish London carriages drew up with crests on their doors and liveried footmen at their boots. Two golden lords and a portly gentleman stepped out. In recent years their sort had rarely been seen even at Wraxham House but never at the rectory.

The lords helped their silken ladies, whether wives or mistresses, Sophie wasn't sure. How was a provincial like herself to tell, except that too colorful clothes and too many feathers adorned them?

They disappeared beneath the portico, thank heaven. But the very sight of London ladies set her to imagining Lionel's former life as one of the ton's acknowledged rakes, tupping trollops, bawds, or mistresses, whose ways she'd learned about reading those erotic books.

Lionel must be an accomplished lover. She didn't doubt it for a minute. But would he have been tender, as the young man she had known, or more forceful, like the men in the books she'd borrowed? Did he do it with mirrors, as one bawdy poem suggested? Or with more than one woman at a time? And what did he have to pay?

He wouldn't have to pay her. Since the night he'd come to her chamber, she'd lain in bed alone reading those borrowed books she'd brought from home and daring herself to go to him.

What was stopping her?

Certainly not innocence, and preserving the reputation she once valued only meant a longer loneliness.

One night she almost made it halfway down the hallway to his suite before she heard a cough. Another early morning, awakened by birdsong at the crack of dawn, she stood before his doors, not knowing which to open, not wanting to find out if they were locked.

Cowardice, that was it, or fear of failure. Because since the night of his unguarded interest in her nipples under that wet dress, he'd been a perfect gentleman. True to his word, to her great disappointment.

Her nerves were raw and jumping from a constant humming awareness of his presence. And a growing worry that she would never learn more about the pleasures between a woman and a man.

"Dr. Roger Fotherington has come from London to examine Simon," Lionel's voice rasped, his warm breath tingling down her neck. Where had he come from? Startled but pleased, she turned to gaze into his solemn gray eyes. The late morning sun showed flecks of iron, steely and determined, a darker side of the lover who intruded upon her imagination.

The lover who wouldn't let her into his.

"A doctor for Simon. But he's been doing so very well."

"That's the problem," Lionel said gravely. "He has seemed to recover before, Sophie, only to take a sudden downturn. Nurse Nesbit urged me to consult Fotherington once again."

"Who is this Dr. Fotherington?"

"The queen's physician, the one I found for Simon after his mother died. He recommends against excitement."

"You mean the one who recommended limiting Simon to easy reading and simple sums," Sophie said, dismayed.

"The very one."

"I think that's utter rubbish. Look at Simon. He's happy as a pig in mud."

Simon's shirt was splattered with the clay he happily sank his hands into.

Lionel scowled at the mess his youngest son had made. "On the contrary, Sophie. He's so absorbed in what he's doing, he looks almost obsessed."

"He's a boy," she protested. "He's *learning*. He's engaged in what he's doing."

Lionel's face shuttered. "Dr. Fotherington is in the library," he said neutrally. "Clean Simon up and bring him to us there. Then you can return to the twins."

Sophie trembled with anger. She was a goose for indulging in dreamy, misplaced fantasies of Simon's father, a man so changed, so closed to new ideas. "You said you entrusted me with his education."

"I do," he said complacently. "But his health is a matter for his physician."

She had no choice, but Simon was still working on the tail of his Trojan horse and didn't want to go. She couldn't blame him. She'd worked the entire week to bring the ancient Greek world to life for the boys, and her efforts and their newfound knowledge were to culminate in tomorrow's show.

Once washed up, Simon trudged alongside her to the library. There, he entered cautiously and stood back from the portly Fotherington. Sophie had the exact same reservations.

The man was genial, however, with great thick gray eyebrows that waggled when he talked. She curtsied, painfully conscious of the gap between their stations. Who was she to question the Physician in Ordinary to the Queen? Meeting him was as close as a rector's daughter might hope to get to any of the royal family. Whereas Lionel was probably on speaking terms with them. The chasm between his class and hers had never seemed so vast, her overheated spinster's fantasies of the earl next door never so ridiculous.

She left the library with relief, but Lionel stopped her in the hallway. "Tell Nurse to arrange an early dinner for the boys. Fotherington is down with friends of mine from London, so you and Miss Upton will want to prepare for something more formal than our family evenings."

Sophie bit off a retort. She had worked so hard to put the boys on a better footing with their distant father. "The children love taking their evening meal with you. They need that time with you."

"But not with guests."

"London guests would give them a chance to practice the manners we have been working on," Sophie argued.

Lionel grimaced. "Sophie, these are friends from my racing, drinking, and gaming days."

"Oh, then I can see where Celia and I will fit right in," Sophie shot back.

Lionel sighed heavily. "Miss Upton knows Deveraux through her father, and her brother married Orlando's sister. My friends aren't clergymen, or saints, Sophie." He gave an exasperated sigh. "It was the only way to get Fotherington down to examine Simon."

"And we both agree what a good idea that is," Sophie said ironically.

"Wait until we hear what he recommends. And come to dinner, Sophie. I expect you to wear your best."

Sophie strode out of the room, muttering to herself. *He* expected her to wear her best! Who did he think he was, ordering her about? Her employer? Her lord?

And yet it pleased her that he insisted that she come and even cared what she would wear.

Pleased her, and worried her. Celia might know Deveraux and Orlando's sister, but Sophie's experience of peers was limited to Lionel and his father.

Dinner that evening was the most lavish affair of Sophie's limited experience.

Thank heaven for Celie, she thought, as she trimmed herself a bite of braised spring lamb à la bourgionette and self-consciously popped it in her mouth.

At least she didn't have to worry about showing her provincial manners. It wasn't difficult to keep your elbows off the table when the sleeves of your only old silk evening dress were faded and frayed and had to be hidden beneath the table-cloth.

But Celia, ah! Her azure dress was stunning, deepening the brilliant sky blue of her eyes. She was in her element, her talents on parade for Lionel's London guests.

Her friend traded bon mots with the flamboyant Lord Deveraux, who positively glittered in his stylish attire.

She swapped fashion tips with Lady Cassandra, who turned out to be his wife.

And she amused the impressive Lord Orlando, who, like Lionel, was an expert whip, and sympathized with his companion, who turned out to be his *sister*. Belinda was a diamond of the first water, more than willing to hold forth on the hazards of navigating impecunious suitors at Almack's.

Sophie hung her head. What uncharitable conclusions about the ladies' virtue she'd leapt to when they'd disembarked from their lords' fancy phaetons. What a bumpkin Lionel would think her if he knew how wretchedly mistaken she had been about his friends.

Celia had made no such mistakes. She even charmed the old doctor with a less than decorous recounting of how her father, squire and magistrate, was surviving his gunshot bum. Dr. Fotherington chortled along with her a few moments, then turned confidingly to Sophie.

"I spoke to Wraxham about young Simon, madam, and wish to inquire more particularly into your present intentions with him," he said softly. But not so softly that Lionel couldn't hear if he so desired.

"Of course, sir," Sophie said. "What is it that you wish to know?"

"His present course of study."

Sophie stiffened. Lionel already objected to her methods, and was sure to side with the doctor. "I advanced him from simple sums to multiplication and from the children's books in English to beginning Latin. He can keep up with his brothers in history and reading, so he now joins them for that."

The doctor gestured for her to go on.

"I can only assure you, sir, that he seems much more settled working with them than when he spent so much time alone."

"Ah," said the doctor. His thick gray eyebrows waggled gravely. "And am I to understand that you read to him before he goes to sleep?"

"Sometimes he reads aloud as well, but yes, when he starts to tire, I read until he drifts off."

"Um." The doctor took a plum from the étagère before them, piled with fresh fruit from the orangery where she'd taken the boys to study nature on a rainy day. "He . . . ah . . . mentioned learning backgammon and chess."

"Yes, sir. He is very quick." She couldn't help smiling. The child's progress made her proud. "Another week or two of practice, and he will start to beat his brothers."

She caught the doctor's speaking glance at Lionel, and then felt the older man's soft hands cup hers. She almost gasped at the unwelcome intimacy.

"I applaud your ingenuity, my dear, and your good intentions. You have never seen another case of the terrors, if I am to understand aright?"

"No, never."

"They can appear seductively simple, but they never are."

She managed a small smile. "There was nothing simple about his terrifying fit."

"No. Quite," the doctor agreed. "They are dreadful for everyone concerned. And we can never know what is going on in the sufferer's overheated brain. Naturally, we want to prevent any recurrence."

"Naturally," she said, aware, too aware, of Lionel's steely gaze.

The doctor went on, oblivious to the undercurrents of discord rippling between her and her employer. "To that end, I have recommended to Lord Wraxham that the regimen I prescribed for Simon be reinstated."

Sophie's heart lurched in protest. Her way was *working*. Perhaps she misunderstood. "And that regimen, sir, would be . . . ?"

"The easy reading, the simple sums, absolute quiet at bedtime, solitude at night to rest his brain."

"That clearly wasn't working, Dr. Fotherington. . . ." She cast a pleading look at Lionel, but his face was set.

"Come, come, my dear," the elderly man said genially. "Will you not allow me my few years' experience over yours?"

Put that way, she had to. He was the queen's physician. She could see how his manner had gained Lionel's confidence. But she was losing what suddenly seemed the most important battle of her life. Certainly of Simon's few short years. "Yes, Doctor, I can, but—"

"But you worry. Of course you do. You are a kind and gentle woman, a woman of sympathy, and I am given to understand, of great learning as well. Naturally you want to impart that to your charges." He was massaging her hand now, as if to persuade her through her pores. His hands were warm, a healer's hands. "And yet . . . will you kindly credit me with my knowledge of these things? Young Master Simon is far from the first child I have treated with these symptoms. In time my patients do recover."

She bowed her head. She had to acknowledge not only his erudition but also the courtesy of his address.

"In all likelihood," he went on, "the symptoms will worsen, again, and perhaps again, before the child recovers."

Because the treatment makes him worse, her heart protested still.

But the doctor, and evidently Lionel, could not hear her heart.

"We—that is, you, as his tutor—will help him take a step back to safer, less arduous tasks. And when his terror recommences, as it surely will, the cold baths will be used to return him to our world."

Celia and the other guests had chattered on gaily without

them, and strangely they burst into laughter just as Dr. Fotherington completed his instructions.

Sophie shot Lionel a desperate look: *Spare your son.*

He closed his eyes as if in pain—but pain for whom? she wondered—and then said, "I fear, Miss Bowerbank, we must bow to the doctor's superior experience. He has clients in London, parents of children just like Simon, who testify to the efficacy of his approach."

She couldn't bring herself to say yes. She looked down at her plate. Bits of sacrificial new spring lamb floated on a bed of peas and cabbage. Tears of vexation threatened to spill over.

"Simon is Lord Wraxham's son," was all she could bring herself to concede.

Banned from helping Simon! Sophie was furious, but defeated. For she had spoken her mind in the strongest terms she dared, and Lionel hadn't listened. She didn't stay to partake of coffee with the women while the men indulged in their port.

She escaped to the library on leaden feet, astonished how much it hurt to abandon Simon to the well-intentioned doctor and the night.

She pulled a worn volume of *The Iliad* from the shelf, thinking to review the siege of Troy, but couldn't concentrate. Rebelling in the one small way remaining to her, she thumbed through the old earl's forbidden books along the highest library shelves.

Ah. There it was.

She plucked down *The Maid's Vindication: or, The Fifteen Comforts of Living a Single Life*, curled up on a damask sofa, and studied its imprecations against men. They should purge her of her foolish fantasies! What a ninnyhammer she was to let a man like Lionel Westfall get a handle on her heart.

Chapter Nine

It tempts us when we see it not,
And makes us flatter, whine and crave;
Yet, when the darling Prize we've got,
The more it yields, the less we have.
—Little Merlin's Cave: A Riddle (1737)

Old habits die hard, Lionel thought. He studied his hand at whist and played his trump card, fingers ever so slightly itching for serious stakes. He'd been too busy with his sons and his new county duties to miss the variety of London, but he missed the rush of risk.

At home the risks were all too real and not of his own choosing. The twins' escapades, Simon's episodes, and his own precarious balance with them and their new tutor—none carried the glamour and excitement he still craved.

Tonight his sons were in bed at last, and Lionel diverted himself from family matters with the mildly amusing task of deciphering Miss Celia Upton's next gambit. His very clever partner was mounting a winning campaign against Orlando's sister and that old shark Fotherington.

Clever at more than cards, Celia had amused his friends and their wife and sister over dinner long enough for Fotherington to confer with Sophie about Simon. Lionel wasn't sure if the old sawbones had convinced his new tutor of the efficacy of his regimen, but she'd clearly understood it.

She would just have to come up to snuff, he thought gloomily.

Nevertheless her defense of Simon had impressed him. If he'd stood by his sons as she was standing up for Simon, none of them would be in the fix they were in today. But he hadn't, and he could not turn back time. He would repair what he had to repair, and go forward as best he could.

The hand went round the table, and again he lost himself in play.

So he was caught unawares when Thomas Beane, the footman standing in for his butler still in London, bent at his ear and whispered urgently, "It's the lad, me lord. 'E's taken another fit."

"Find Miss Bowerbank," Lionel ordered. She would better understand how to help his son if she saw Dr. Fotherington at work. But he dreaded the scene he knew awaited them for the child, for her, and for himself. He laid his cards facedown on the table and hastily made his excuses.

Fotherington folded his hand too and stood. "My regrets, ladies. Duty calls."

Nurse Nesbit, back from her ailing parent's side, had Simon pinned to his little cot, just as Dr. Fotherington instructed. A chambermaid stood by, wringing her hands at the awful struggle. Heartsick, Lionel watched the poor child flail and gasp for breath, his anguished face contorted in terror.

Lionel fought his memories. He would not be caught out again as Sophie had seen him, powerless to help his son. He could only hope Fotherington knew what he was proposing. Could only hope that Sophie could accept it, with her strong opinions and already too strong connection to the boy. Which . . . where was Sophie, anyway? Hadn't he told Beane to hurry?

"Ready for the water, Wraxham," Fotherington announced, intruding on his thoughts. Lionel sent the chambermaid to summon footmen with cold water from the bottom of the deepest well. In minutes Simon's copper tub was full. Clenching his jaw against his own horrors, Lionel helped Nurse remove Simon's nightshirt. Determined to master himself, he set himself to do the dousing too. Yes, the dousing was harsh, but after everything that had been tried and had been worse, if this didn't work, what would?

"You in your fine clothes, my lord?" Nesbit said heartily, bracing Simon's struggling body above the icy water. "Nay, I've done it afore, and it's what ye pay me for."

Sophie strode into the room, horror on her face. "What in the world do you think you're doing, Nesbit?"

"Ah, Miss Bowerbank," Fotherington said, unruffled as if instructing a class of green apprentices in London. "Good of you to join us. As you will see in just a moment, it serves no purpose to delay the cold bath at a time like this."

She whirled on Lionel. "I cannot countenance this, my lord. You cannot."

He didn't, but he desperately wanted to do the right thing.

"Trust me, Sophie, if there was any other way we'd do it."

Her pretty mouth was pressed in a thin line of mutinous dissent.

Simon's pale limbs struggled against Nesbit's sturdy body, but she lowered him straightaway. His soles touched the icy water first, and a plaintive scream pierced the dimly lit nursery . . . and Lionel's soldier's heart.

God, how he despised this. But dousing Simon had worked before, and more quickly than Penelope's crueler measures.

Fotherington stepped up to the tub. "That's right, you see, my lord, Miss Bowerbank, this is how it's done. Slowly. Good, Nesbit, very good. Lower." He swung his great gray head around to check on Sophie, water splashing everywhere.

Lionel looked at her too. She'd pressed her knuckles to her teeth in an agony of empathy with his poor son.

"Just a few more moments, Miss Bowerbank," the doctor said, dispassionate but kind. "We want to shock the whole body to break the hold of his fears."

"You mean, to break his spirit and his heart," Lionel heard Sophie mutter. Grimly, he set his mind against yielding to her plea. She couldn't know. He loathed the doctor's regimen, but he'd searched high and low for any better one, and Fotherington was the only man he'd found who didn't think the child possessed and believed that he'd get better.

Simon's legs and arms churned in the water, soaking the nurse and splashing everyone nearby. Excruciating long minutes ticked by. Simon's screams trailed into soft sobs, and his body slumped, as the doctor had foretold. Nesbit lifted him dripping from the water into the maid's waiting towel.

Faster than they could resist or Lionel could act, Sophie wrested the boy and towel from them, stalked to the nearby rocker, and claimed his son as hers.

Fotherington hastened over, disguising his displeasure with practiced courtesy. "You spoil our outcome, Miss Bowerbank, by coddling the boy and overexciting his unquiet mind. You must leave him alone now."

Through tears of defiance, Sophie looked straight past the doctor at Lionel. "I will not let him go."

"Sophie . . ." Lionel spread his hands in appeal. "The doctor has experience in these cases. He has come from London expressly to advise us."

"He may advise all he wishes. I will not leave this child."

The doctor's face went red. "Madam, you forget my position. I predicted the return of Master Simon's fits, and so they have returned. I promised the bath would be effective, and the fit has broken."

She clearly gave up on the doctor. "Of course his fits returned, my lord. Having company disrupted his routine."

The doctor sputtered. "Generally, madam, such patients

have fits at random intervals regardless of whether they are kept to a routine. But they always respond to the bath."

"On the contrary, my lord, Simon's episodes usually end within the hour, bath or no, which makes me question the efficacy of your baths."

Blast. Much as Lionel hated the procedure, he'd not made that connection. He made it now. "My good doctor, Miss Bowerbank, whatever the reason, Simon has grown quieter, which is all any of us wanted. Let us not quarrel in front of him whether he hears us or not."

"I repeat, madam," said the doctor, apparently unwilling to retreat before a mere gentlewoman, "you must leave him alone now."

Sophie's face set in defiant pride, a look Lionel had last seen on the fated day that summer their fathers had torn them apart. "I will abide by Lord Wraxham's orders," she said, but did not release his son.

"Thank you, Sophie," Lionel said. "And, Doctor, it is very late, and you must be tired. Beane here can show you to your room, and I will deal with Miss Bowerbank."

Huffing about intractable upstart female staff, the portly doctor made his exit behind the lanky footman.

Lionel closed the door behind them and gathered his wits for battle. Just now, he hated insurrection, arrogance, and women, but not in that order.

He didn't know how to deal with Sophie as an employee.

He didn't know how to deal with her attachment to his son.

Least of all did he know how to deal with her confidence that she was right. He had to admire her stand. If he'd had that confidence, so much might have been different between him and the six strangers of his loins. He was a rogue, a cad, a bounder not to have done better by his sons and by her.

"Shhh, my lord," he heard her whisper from the rocking chair.

Her sudden shift, the gentleness, unmanned him. He padded lightly across the floor and pulled up a stool beside the woman he'd once loved and his son by a woman who'd despised him. To his surprise, he did not love Simon the less for being born of his first wife.

Simon instinctively wrapped his arms around Sophie's neck and burrowed in, his breathing regular and his wet hair drying into a dark halo around his head.

Tears damped Sophie's sable lashes, and fatigue made dark smudges below her eyes.

"He's almost asleep, the poor darling," she said softly, pushing back a stray tendril from Simon's peaceful face.

The tenderness in her tired smile almost broke Lionel's heart. Penelope had never bathed her sons in such a light of love. *His* sons. Their mother had never cared for them like that.

Nor had he, not in word or deed.

Then Sophie added simply, "You will have to discharge me, my lord, before I will allow anyone to put him through such tortures again."

He covered her free hand with his, touched beyond the telling at her implacable revolt. "I may have to," he said hoarsely.

She blinked, obviously expecting better of him.

Under her influence, he was coming to expect better of himself. It was just such a long journey from having been father in name only to becoming father to his sons in deed, in life, in heart.

"Discharge me, my lord?"

"It might come to that," he said perversely. He just hadn't found the words yet to say that he'd been wrong as only a misguided rakehell could be.

"Ah," she said, her eyes closing while her lips curved at his irony. "Then I would have to call you out."

Perhaps she should, if he could not get it right with such a helpmate at his side.

*　　*　　*

And just what would the esteemed Dr. Fotherington prescribe for her condition? Sophie wondered wryly, feeling the loss when Lionel left the room. Simon at last slept soundly. She tucked him under his covers and returned to her bedroom to huddle under hers for a few short hours of sleep. Every night under Lionel's roof, sleep had been far to seek.

She worried that she'd been too forward with him tonight, was vexed that she hadn't been forward enough. It was proving difficult in a crisis to keep her feelings for her employer separate from her feelings for the man.

But afterward, ah, afterward.

His scent clung to the back of her hand where he had held it. His image danced before her eyes, his scarred brow now arched and questioning, now softening for her. For her. Could it be? She wrapped her arms around her body, wishing she could taste his kisses, feel his breath upon her neck, hear his voice rasping at her ear.

It was too late to look at any of her books. With Lionel singing in her senses, they weren't what she wanted tonight.

"These are back from the bankers, my lord," Barnaby Tims said to Lionel in his office the next morning. The obsequious secretary had pinioned him for business between a hasty breakfast and a meeting with Deveraux and Orlando for that ultimate in gentlemanly rustifications, the shooting match.

Tims laid the revised mortgage notes and bills of sale on the desk before him and neatened up the edges with long flat white fingers.

"Hurry about it then," Lionel said, feeling cross and tired. What with whist, cold baths, and hot, unwelcome thoughts about Simon's fierce new advocate, he'd slept little and rested less.

Lionel checked the terms grimly. By divesting himself of the hunting box in Hampshire, he could just make the next quarter. As to any increase in income needed to restore Wraxham's former glory, he would have to further reduce the stables and improve his tenants' dwindling harvests. But those were matters to take up with his estate agent Carter, which would further alienate Tims, who resented Carter's taking over responsibilities that had once been his.

Bugger estate politics, Lionel thought, heading down the hall for the gun room, where Deveraux and Orlando awaited him. Good. He needed to shoot something.

A distant ruckus—from the front portico?—suggested his chance was coming sooner rather than later. Exasperated, he broke into a run. When he'd stepped in as magistrate, he hadn't anticipated the aggravation of local squabbles landing at his doorstep.

A clash of angry voices crescendoed as he neared.

"You've got no proof, man." It sounded like Carter. What the devil was his estate agent doing in local dustups?

"The past is proof enough for me," came a stranger's voice.

Lionel pushed through the doors. Carter was nose to nose with Robert Roscoe, Squire Upton's steward, a compact, competent little man, evenhanded in his affairs.

"Anyone could have let those goats out," Carter said indifferently, his usual arrogance on full display. "Your stable boy, a milkmaid."

"Not on my watch, they wouldn't," Roscoe fumed.

"Good morning, Mr. Roscoe," Lionel interrupted. "Carter. I take it one of you has a matter for the acting magistrate."

Roscoe doffed his hat. "Your Lordship, no. I mean, a matter for you, my lord, not as magistrate."

"As father, my lord," Carter inserted.

Lionel's breath hitched, but he said smoothly, "Ah. My sons." Not Simon, of course. But the twins . . .

Roscoe gulped, then rushed ahead. "With all due respect, my lord, the squire's good spring garden's been chewed up, the goats let out, and Lady Upton's prized topiary devoured."

Lionel saw Lady Upton's spindly, bizarre collection of animals sculpted from shrubbery every time he held another session at the Grange. It would be a mercy for the goats to rid the countryside of Lady Upton's outlandish affectation. He forced gravity. "This is a serious charge, Roscoe. My man Carter has a point about that proof."

Roscoe ran his hat brim through his fingers. "Well, here's how I see it, my lord, and if you don't mind my saying so, the squire, 'e's of the same opinion. Our goats have never gotten out afore. We know goats, and we pen 'em behind a double latch."

Lionel suppressed an urge to reach for his snuffbox. The trivial—the solvable—complications of London life felt very far away. "So you think my boys sneaked out at night, found your goat pen, opened your double latch in the dark, and somehow persuaded the goats to go and ruin the gardens, Lady Upton's topiary in particular?"

"Yes, my lord. Sir. We think it's highly probable."

"On the grounds of . . ."

"The whole village saw what they did to the poor Misses Gatewoods' sheets."

Lionel was glad he'd had a few afternoons on the bench. He'd cultivated an intimidating restraint.

"Indeed."

"Nothing like this ever happened before they came to live here."

"Nothing . . ." Lionel said stonily.

Roscoe stepped back. "On this scale, my lord."

"Carter has a point, though, about proof."

Roscoe crushed the brim of his hapless hat. "Proof?"

"Do you have any proof? Someone must have seen something suspicious, something left behind. Footprints. A glove."

"It's a terrible scene, my lord, destruction everywhere."

"In other words, no."

"Yes, my lord, no. No proof, that is, my lord. Yet."

There was nothing for it but to take decisive action. "Carter, my guests are in the gun room, ready for a shooting party. You know where to take them. I'll go over to the squire's and assess the damage. Ready, Roscoe?"

*   *   *

It was worse than Roscoe's dark account had led him to expect, Lionel thought. His bad knee ground against itself as he traipsed around the twisted and broken limbs of the once orderly geometrical green figures, clipped and pruned and shaped to within an inch of their lives.

He'd been looking for proof for half an hour and finding nothing but destruction.

Squire Upton, only slightly better able to walk than sit, shuffled painfully alongside Lionel, snorting in indignation at each new insult to his wife's dignity. He paused before an unrecognizable shape, nothing but broken twigs and strewn leaves now.

"That stork was her favorite. I planted it to celebrate our daughter's birth. The rest, they were presents, for birthdays, anniversaries, some such . . ."

"I didn't realize," Lionel said, achieving a sympathetic tone, he hoped, despite standing in the most frivolous formal garden in all Europe. The most frivolous ruined formal garden in all Europe.

"Damned vandals. And I don't mean the goats."

"You mean my twins," he said pointedly, irked that the man beat about the bushes.

"It's too bad they started out on the wrong foot with the sheets. But yes, my lord, they were the first culprits we thought of."

"I'll not punish them without proof."

Squire Upton nodded. "We'll keep looking for it, not that I'm out to get them."

"Not that I'm out to get them off the hook, but I will do the looking. After I question them."

"Fair enough," the squire said, kicking a clump of greenery out of the graveled path. "It isn't just the cost, my lord, or the years it took to cultivate. This was my wife's pride and pleasure."

Lionel turned on his heel and headed for his phaeton, wishing he could take pride and pleasure in his sons.

Back at Wraxham House, Lionel sent for Sophie to come to his office, rather than risk the tirade against Maxim and Alexander that was building in him. He hoped like bloody hell they had done nothing, but neither Upton nor his steward was the kind of man to point a finger at innocents.

His knee throbbed too much for him to pace away his anger and impatience. So he sat and thought of Sophie.

"It's too early to dismiss me, my lord," she said, rushing in, her nut-brown hair streaming over her shoulders.

Dismissing her was the last thing on his mind.

Pressing her into a corner and kissing her, on the other hand, until she writhed and plunged beneath him and he was emptying his frustrations and his passions into her welcome warmth . . . that almost overtook his worry about the twins.

"I deserve a chance to prove myself," she went on when she caught her breath. "Last night I may have spoken out of line, but Simon needs me, and the twins, and I believe I can do them a world of—"

"You're not dismissed," Lionel said, pressing two fingers to her lips to stop the flow of self-justification. He fought a swell of gratitude for both her apology and her dedication. He fought another, lower, untoward, inconvenient swell.

Damn.

"We have another problem. Please, sit."

She took an upright chair and sat, that tumble of dark hair playing temptingly about her face, her bosom heaving with agitated breaths of worry.

He sat too, and forced his gaze elsewhere, but it rested on the charming blush that rushing here had left upon her chest and throat and cheeks. She looked like a woman just come from making love.

"It's my father, isn't it?"

Wresting his attention away from her with an effort, he explained the devastation at Squire Upton's.

She calmed her ragged breathing. "How dreadful. Celia's mother worshipped her topiary. What does Celia say?"

Lionel hadn't given Sophie's companion a thought. "I don't know if she's been told."

Sophie popped up and headed for the door. "She should hear straightaway."

"Sophie, not yet," he called out after her. "Celia's father, and Robert Roscoe too, suspect the twins."

"No." Sophie sat back down with a defeated plop. "They've been with me all morning."

"The damage happened in the night."

She shook her head as if she couldn't believe it. "Everyone was with Simon last night," she said gravely.

Which would have left the twins unsupervised. Lionel had had that selfsame thought. "That doesn't mean they even left their room."

"Or that they stayed there either."

He scowled, not so much at her as at the turn his thoughts had taken. Good God, they'd had time, opportunity. "Upton has no evidence that they did it."

"And we have no proof they didn't."

"Worse yet, the first thing he and his steward remembered was those blasted sheets."

"This is so much more awful, though. Permanent destruction, as you describe it. But still . . ." She went silent, thinking God knew what.

"What have you seen, Sophie?"

Her eyes slid away from his. "It's nothing, truly."

"Truly," Lionel said, clenching his jaw.

"They've done nothing so very bad," she said, championing his sons as if they needed to be protected from him.

"You must be honest with me, Sophie. You spend more time with them than anyone."

She wrung her hands. "Yes, but . . ."

"But what?" he pressed, impatience growing. And worry too. "I can't be a better father if you leave me in the dark."

"Very well then, but I am only beginning to earn their trust. If they feel that I am running to you over every little incident, telling tales, I will lose that trust."

He pushed his fingers through his hair, stifling a sharp retort. He'd never had their trust, and he was questioning the wisdom of entrusting her.

"And my trust, Sophie? You are responsible to me as well as them."

She smoothed her skirts over the tops of her thighs, a nervous, private gesture that even in the tension of the moment socked him in the gut with its latent sensuality and then roused him. Damn, damn, damn. So much for reform. He'd be a rake to the bloody end.

"They do so love a good prank, my lord. Clever, mischievous pranks."

"Limited to the schoolroom, I trust."

She winced becomingly. "Actually, my lord, they're quite inventive."

He started to stand to tower over her, but doing so would reveal the inconvenient direction of his other interests.

"Sophie!" he commanded. "Tell."

"It's rather a long list."

He lounged in his chair, took refuge in his snuffbox, and listened to her spell out their pranks and peccadilloes.

Between hiding chalk, rearranging books, and shifting tables when she'd stepped out of the schoolroom, they'd led her a merry chase. She'd handled it by keeping spare chalk in her pockets, by never showing surprise, and especially by never putting anything back to rights that inconvenienced them.

She told her tale with a relish for meeting the twins' challenges and defeating them underhandedly. They'd been busy little buggers, but her enthusiasm for matching wits with them reminded him of a younger Sophie and touched him in places he did not quite want touched.

"I thought I'd gained the upper hand," she ended solemnly. "But then strange things started happening to my room."

"To your bedchamber," he clarified.

She blushed surprisingly red and gave an awkward nod.

He leaned forward, biting back a rude oath aimed at his little blighters. "Go on."

"My hairbrush would not be where I'd left it on the vanity. My dresses in the wardrobe showed up in a different order. This morning, my hose were torn."

White-hot anger swept him, and then a bleak black disappointment settled in. He stood and looked out his window, his unruly lust—and his frustrations over Sophie—momentarily under control. "This can't be Max and Alex. Bright and mischievous, yes. They've been that almost from the cradle. But not malicious. Never malicious."

"I do credit them with the schoolroom pranks, my lord. But the invasion of my . . . privacy . . . It lacks a certain, I don't know how to say it, boyishness. Yes, boyishness, and daring."

"I will have the lock on your door reset."

Short of standing sentinel, it was the best he could do. In fact, given his perpetual state of arousal anywhere in her vicinity, standing sentinel was probably about the most dangerous service he could offer her.

"That would be kind, my lord."

"I will have to investigate the garden incident further, and then confront them."

"I should like to accompany you, my lord."

"I don't see the point."

She gave him a small smile. "As the butt of their previous pranks, I might see something."

He nodded his agreement. He didn't really think spending more time in her presence was advisable, for him and this growing hunger, but he believed she wanted the best for his sons, and he believed she wanted to help him rule them out.

106

Chapter Ten

Sweet pretty Babes, the Product of each Charm,
In Marriage-Bed protects us from all harm,
Their Innocence like Lambs and Doves appear,
Which make our Hearts and Minds quite void of Care.
—The Batchelors and Maids Answer to the
Fifteen Comforts of Matrimony (1706?)

Sophie surveyed Lady Upton's shattered garden, shivering. Her dress was too light for such a day, and her slippers too thin to walk outdoors. Luckily Lionel's tall broad form sheltered her from a stiff spring breeze.

"I don't believe goats would do this, my lord."

He scowled at the trampled ground. "Those cloven hoof-prints are too small for cattle."

"Oh, the goats were here, no doubt about it. But they don't destroy things at random."

A corner of his mouth quirked, plunging her into memories of easier, more frequent smiles.

"You do not strike me as a goatherd, Sophie. Nor is the rectory a proper farm."

"I had pets once," she reminded him.

I had you once, younger and not so severe.

Their footsteps crunched along the gravel walk, his solid and determined, hers lighter, more vulnerable. Once they had wandered Wraxham's fields and gardens, so like these, talking and then seeking privacy for more wanton explorations. She wished she were so fortunate now, showered with love and hot sensation.

With effort, she came back to the matter at hand. "When goats graze shrubbery and trees, they stand on their hind legs to nibble at the leaves. They don't tear branches off tree trunks."

Broken cypress limbs littered the winding walk. Lionel took her elbow with a steadying hand and stepped her over them. His touch sent tingles up her arm.

"There, see?" She pointed to a particularly mangled limb. "That used to be a teapot. Silly, really, in a garden."

"At least we agree on that."

"But its spout and handle were ripped off, the branch torn from the trunk."

He picked up the ruined branch and examined it, looking as if his heart had been ripped out too. "Someone more than let those goats loose. Someone led them here, destroyed the garden, and left the goats to take the blame."

"Someone, my lord?"

"My sons could have done it. We know they could have."

She didn't think so. Not now. Not after seeing the vicious damage firsthand.

Whoever did this had a personal grudge.

"Mischief against me I can understand, perhaps even the mischief in my chamber. They don't want a tutor, especially a woman. But why mayhem against Squire Upton? When I caught them throwing stones at the Misses Gatewoods' sheets, you were the magistrate who punished them."

"And I will be the one to investigate this and question them. As magistrate, but even more as their father."

The reluctance in his voice spoke volumes. He didn't want to blame his boys. But he clearly felt compelled to consider their guilt before anyone else's.

"You have to question others too. Anyone could have done this," Sophie insisted.

"No one has accused more likely culprits," he said dryly.

"Which doesn't mean there aren't any. Squire Upton has been the magistrate for years. His judgments could have put any number of people's noses out of joint."

"He swears that nothing like this happened before I moved my family back from London."

"That could be coincidence, my lord."

"Or not. Good God, Sophie. Do you think I want to find my own sons guilty? I will look for proof, not that they did it, but that they did not. And I'll begin by talking with them."

"I would like to be there when you do."

"To what end?"

"As their tutor. As their victim. Even as the one who found them stoning sheets."

His gray eyes darkened. "That won't be necessary."

"But I—"

"This is something I must do myself. Something my sons and I must do together."

She started to argue her point but thought better of it. He did need to do things with his sons, in good times and even more in bad.

Sophie checked herself before the mirror in her chamber, desperate to restore a semblance of order before dinner with Lionel and his noble guests. The blue silk was worn and old, fitting for the family's tutor, and so acceptable. But the afternoon sun had reddened her face, the wind had tangled her ungovernable hair, and her blood still pulsed because . . .

Admit it, she admonished herself. Her blood pulsed because

109

she'd spent a thrilling afternoon with Lionel unchaperoned, casting reputation to the wind in the urgency of solving the mystery of the marauding goats.

She took up a comb and started working out the tangles, ends first. He'd driven her the couple of furlongs to Upton Grange and back in his phaeton. With apparent disregard for her astonishment, he'd pushed his fashionable bays at a spanking pace, wheeling them round corners and whipping them to a flat-out gallop on stretches of straight road.

As he must have learned to do in London.

Where he'd been a noted whip and storied rake.

She broke a tooth on a nasty snarl. That long-ago summer the lad she'd known had only walked with her, or rather ambled and meandered through the fields. She'd been no more prepared for his fashionable expertise with carriages than for his exhilarating recklessness with speed.

His dash, his utter manliness, took her breath away. And when his long, caressing fingers softly spoke to his horses through the reins, she'd imagined other caresses, stolen ones.

Promised ones.

Denied ones.

She pulled her hair into a proper bun. The earl of Wraxham was her employer, she told herself. The earl and the rector's daughter were worlds apart. His children were her charges. Except for that wild ride, he'd acted as the most circumspect escort, intent on the criminals and the crime.

So her sizzling, swirling, painful desire to take him as a lover was . . . painful. Futile.

She powdered her red nose and rosy cheeks and headed down for dinner.

When Sophie finally had an opportunity to tell Celia about her mother's topiary, her friend burst into tears. Sophie had repaired herself as best she could and joined with Lionel's guests in the drawing room before going in to dinner. Celia's display took Sophie by surprise. If Celia hadn't made sport of her mother's silly garden for donkey's years, Sophie might have given more credit to her tears.

Even so, she excused her friend. Who wouldn't be cut up over the wanton violation of her childhood home?

But Sophie would have felt more sympathetic if Celia's tears hadn't played so directly to a bored, restless, *unwed* Lord Orlando.

"Dastardly deed, whoever done it, Miss Upton," he said, exuding empathy in smart London slang.

Celia sniffled prettily, dabbing the tears that ran alongside her pert, perfect nose and down her modestly rouged cheeks. "Sorry to be such a watering pot, my lord. But my mother so adored her garden."

Celia's tearful display rankled Sophie. Celia was *her* companion, not vice versa, and Sophie was the tutor whose charges were running wild.

"They should put thumb screws to the vandals that done it, that's my humble opinion," Lord Orlando was saying in Wraxham House's elegant yellow drawing room.

Sophie nearly choked. She doubted there was a humble opinion in His Lordship's least left toe.

Celia fluttered her damp lashes. "You are severe, my lord. Transportation is the punishment I'd levy on them. Give the lads a chance to start somewhere afresh."

Lads? Sophie thought, alarmed. The more alarmed because Lionel had just strolled in and had to overhear.

What must he think?

Did Celia know something she and Lionel had missed?

"It could have been vagrants or Gypsies, Celie, not lads necessarily," Sophie pointed out.

Celia smiled past the tears glistening in her golden lashes. "Of course, Sophie dearest. But it would have been someone of the male persuasion, don't you agree?"

Sophie almost laughed with relief. She was overly apprehensive, her judgment shot, her nerves on end from too much of Lionel.

"In all probability, yes, a man, although it's hard for me to imagine even the meanest ruffian having so little fellow feeling."

"You must not have spent much time in London, Miss Bowerbank," Lord Orlando said loftily.

Lionel's hand touched the small of her back in secret support. "Miss Bowerbank has, I believe, spent no time in London, which accounts for her sweet temper and her sanguine hopes for the criminal classes."

Sophie felt her face heat. Yes, it was a social liability to have no experience of London. Not only had she lived her entire life in the country, she had never even visited that grand city, making her a rustic twice over.

But Lionel had called her sweet and optimistic with obvious approval.

Sophie didn't recover her equanimity until long after everyone was seated for another formal dinner. Its only saving grace was the absence of Dr. Fotherington. "Fled back to London where he's sure of patients who are obedient, even worshipful," Lionel had said, driving her back home in the afternoon.

The meal had ended late, and the London ladies, citing the relaxing properties of the country air, had retired early. Celia, evidently crestfallen to miss out on another late night tête-à-tête with the unwed Lord Orlando, had trudged off to bed.

Or perhaps Celia's tears for her mother had been real, Sophie thought, trying to do her friend justice as she made her way to Simon's room. With Dr. Fotherington gone, she felt obligated to check on the child before she went to bed.

On impulse, she knocked at the door to Celia's suite. If Celia was worried for her mother, she should go home to be with her.

"May I come in?" Sophie asked.

No answer. "Celie, it's Sophie, on a private matter."

In a moment, Celia let her in, visibly brighter than when

Lionel's guests retired. "A private matter? Oh, Sophie, I do so love a secret. Come into my boudoir."

With a twist of her bejeweled hand, she gestured at the most elegant, feminine bedchamber Sophie had ever seen.

Sophie's wine-dark quarters were masculine, drab as her own mousy hair and frumpy form.

Celia's room enhanced her delicate blond beauty. Luxurious damask curtains lined the outside wall, Chinese paper clad the others, and gauzy silks draped her bed as in an exotic Bedouin tent. And there on an inner wall was the Vermeer Celia so admired.

Celia glided across the pastel-figured Turkish carpet to return to her toilette. "His Lordship was terribly kind to allow me Lady Penelope's suite. It's elegant, don't you think?"

Sophie bit her tongue in a mortifying fit of jealousy.

"Of course, our fathers were friends for ages," Celia rattled on, applying a scented cream to cheeks that needed nothing.

He'd given her the late countess's private suite. Their fathers had been friends for ages.

What if Celia and Lionel . . . Lionel and Celia . . . ?

Why else would he have allowed her—no, purposefully *installed* her—in the late Lady Penelope's suite?

The room was worthy of a countess, no doubt about it, and Celia had all the airs and the attributes to be Lionel's next countess. No doubt about that either. A convenient local lass, a family friend, conversant with London society, and yet not without means, or rather, property.

Adjacent property.

How apt. How appalling.

In a fog of lust for Lionel, Sophie had almost overlooked it, deluding herself by watching Celia's hot flirtation with Lord Orlando.

Lord Orlando, Lord Wraxham.

Celia still had the beauty and the manners to attract any man she wanted.

Savagely Sophie repressed the green worm of envy.

113

Celia was her friend, she reminded herself.

Celia had forgiven, oh, the worst a woman could do to another woman.

But what if . . .

No. Lionel was barely in his second month of mourning, even if, as Sophie suspected, his grief was only theoretical.

And Lord Orlando, she had to hope, was on the prowl.

"Celia," Sophie began gravely.

"You really should try this cream, Sophie."

Celia offered a small porcelain jar. Sophie tried not to be offended at the implication that she needed it.

"Celia, I'm not here about that. It's about your mother. Under the circumstances, I thought you might want to return home for a day or two."

Celia's brow, gleaming from the cream, creased. "The circumstances?"

"To comfort your mother."

"And leave you alone?"

"I don't feel alone. The house is full of guests."

Celia was silent for so long that Sophie could almost hear her think. Perhaps she didn't want to leave Lord Orlando, and Sophie was right to suspect she'd set her sights on him. Or perhaps, and more unnerving, Celia didn't want to miss a chance to parade her drawing room manners to Lionel before his friends.

Sophie bit her tongue.

"I would just get in the way of the investigation," Celia finally said.

"Such as it is," Sophie said glumly.

"How is it coming?"

"They've turned up no evidence, nothing conclusive."

"Really." Celia waved off the remark. Her best diamond still adorned the ring finger on her left hand. "I'm sure you're right, dearest. Gypsies, or vagrants."

Sophie groaned. There was no hope for it but to plunge right in. "As a matter of fact," she said, plunging, "your father and Mr. Roscoe suspect the twins."

Celia's pretty pink lips pursed into an O of astonishment. "No!" she added, frowning in evident disbelief. "Oh. His Lordship must be distraught. Or rather, furious. I can't imagine which. Whatever can I say to assure him that we—that I—hold no grudges . . . or do we?" she dithered. "Of course, we don't. They're just boys."

"We have no proof of any kind, either implicating or exonerating them."

"Ah."

"His Lordship, as magistrate, must respect your father's suspicions and look into them. As a father, naturally, he doesn't want to believe it, and will do so only when confronted with the most compelling proof."

"Of course." Celia took off her ring, kissed it, and put it in its velvet box.

Sophie cringed at the reminder of Ewan Ramsay, who'd chosen her over Celia. Sophie had refused him, and he'd gone off to war and died. But that was oh, so far behind them.

"What have the boys to say for themselves?" Celia went on.

Sophie didn't know. "His Lordship is talking to them now. In the morning I will find out what they had to say for themselves."

"They seem very clever, those boys."

Sophie groaned. "Indeed," she said, but she wasn't about to describe their classroom stunts to Celia, much less the mysterious breaches of her chamber.

"Clever enough to have pulled off such a stunt?" she asked, in her breathy whisper.

"Perhaps, but not mean enough," Sophie said, but a pang of doubt stabbed her.

"His Lordship will be relieved then, don't you think?"

"No, Celie, I think His Lordship is devastated that his sons are under suspicion and wracked with despair to think that the suspicions might be true."

Celia's brow furrowed. "Do you mean that he suspects them too?"

"I'm sure he doesn't want to."

Celia crossed her dainty hands over her perfect, and perfectly adorned, bosom. "Oh, how he must be suffering."

What posturing. Sophie reminded herself once again that Celia Upton had been her friend for ages, that they'd played cards together, read and discussed the same books, and shared the choicest roles in Shakespeare's plays for Thursday evening readings.

"On the contrary," Sophie said, "he's a grown man, experienced in the ways of the world. It's the boys my heart goes out to. Suspected at the drop of a hat for something they likely never even thought of. That's the crime, poor things."

Celia patted Sophie's hand. "Of course, you're right, Sophie dearest, to side with the boys. That's what His Lordship hired you for. It's his place to follow any trail of suspicion and either clear them or punish them."

Sophie left Celia's room and headed for Simon's, her head in a swim. She and Lionel both sided with the twins, didn't they? They both believed them innocent, and had set about to prove it, hadn't they?

She paused at the twins' room, wanting to offer them her support. Her hand was on the door latch when she detected the low rumble of their father's voice.

Did he sound angry, accusatory, censuring?

She could not be sure, but she wanted desperately to know.

Because she cared for them. Each and every one.

Her hand paused above the latch. She could just enter, as tutor, on grounds of tucking the boys in. He had insisted that she do that. Her heart thudded with indecision. Lionel had claimed this duty for himself, not the tucking in but the talking-to, and she shouldn't interrupt him during what would at best be a painful and difficult interview.

No matter how much she had come to care. No, the better

part of wisdom was to let it go. In the morning she could talk it over with the boys. Lifting her branch of candles, she stole into Simon's room next door. It was dark as a tomb, filled with the scary, brooding quiet that Dr. Fotherington had ordered and nothing of comfort. She crossed the carpet to Simon's little bed, a soft circle of light from her branch of candles surrounding him. He looked small, frail, exposed. She carefully sat the branch on a bedside table, and bent her knees to sit beside him on the bed.

He moaned and pulled up a fist to rub the dark circle beneath an eye. He was deeply, soundly sleeping.

She touched his shoulder lightly, exactly opposite the doctor's orders, but she couldn't stop herself. Yes, it was late; yes, he appeared to be sleeping peacefully; yes, she was disturbing him. But he needed a soft voice, a loving touch, a gentle story. He needed not to be alone in the black hour when his darkest dreams most often erupted on him.

This she believed, no matter what Dr. Fotherington's vaunted experience told him.

"Simon, sweeting," she whispered.

His face scrunched drowsily.

"It's Miss Bowerbank, Simon, come to say good night just as I promised I would. Would you like to hear a story?"

His eyes fluttered open. "I'd like a sip of water, miss, if you please."

Her heart squeezed, and her eyes teared. What a thoughtful gentleman this dear sweet child would grow up to be. If she could just help him past these childhood terrors. In fact, she'd been thinking what to do about his fear of snakes. A pet snake might just do the trick. And she knew the rascals to find one for her.

She took up an ewer from his low nightstand and poured a crystal-cut tumblerful.

Simon drank greedily, his gray eyes peeking over the round rim of glass. He handed it back to her. "Thank you, ma'am."

"More, my sweet?"

117

He shook his fine dark curls. "I should very much like a song."

Mercy. She was better at stories. She knew hardly any songs for children, remnants of bedtime rhymes her mother must have sung to her and she'd not heard or sung since.

"A lullaby?" she asked.

His perfect bob of a nose wrinkled in boyish disgust. "A *song* song. I'm too old for lullabies."

There was one song. She and Celia had learned a setting for Ariel's ditty from *The Tempest* to perform one Thursday evening. Sung slowly enough and softly, it should do. She closed her eyes and began to hum, stretching her memory for the words, only to feel Simon's matchstick arms encircle her neck and smell his little-boy freshness nuzzled up against her chest.

"More please," he murmured when she paused.

Her heart melted. She carried him to the rocker, settled in with him curled up on her lap, and sang softly. His fine, tousled hair brushed beneath her chin so sweetly that her voice broke, but she quickly cleared her throat and continued on to the end of the song and through it three more times. When she stopped, Simon's thin chest was rising and falling with the quiet steady breaths of a boy in peaceful slumber.

Slowly and inescapably, despair engulfed her, and she felt a great black hole of emptiness where her heart should be.

Deny it though she might, she had missed having children of her own.

She had missed marriage, and not just the erotic passions that plagued her fantasies.

She had missed out on love, pure, selfless, unconditional love.

Lionel found them in the rocker, woman and child, not mother and child, but sweeter than any mother his poor son had ever known.

Except that Sophie shouldn't be here.

If he took Fotherington at his word, it was dangerously wrong to disturb Simon in the night. Simon was supposed to be spared light at night, and sheltered from mental excitation.

Lionel wouldn't even have found them save for the lilt of Sophie's gentle alto.

On his first step into the room, Sophie stopped her song and lifted her gaze, her chin resting lightly on the crown of his son's head.

"What did Max and Alex have to say, my lord?" she whispered.

Lionel, damn it. Here if anywhere, in the bosom of my family.

He lowered his voice too. "They deny everything."

"Everything?"

"The goats, the topiary, the vegetable garden, and most especially anything to do with Miss Bowerbank's boudoir. They didn't even find it funny."

In fact, they'd protested vehemently, and he'd grilled them more like the military officer he'd once been than the caring father he aspired to be. And if he'd hated that job then over green lads pressed into service fresh from the countryside, he loathed it over his own privileged and yet vulnerable sons.

She exhaled in relief. "So there you have it, my lord."

No, he had nothing.

No proof the twins were innocent, no guarantee his youngest son would have a peaceful night, no confidence in his role as father, no compliance from their tutor, and no control over his randy raging body.

Because in the midst of his family's chaos, Sophie still aroused him. He couldn't be sure if it was her womanly tenderness toward Simon or the warm, sensual glow of her flawless skin bathed in the golden candlelight.

But he fought seeing her in yet another favorable perspective.

"You should not be here," he said bluntly.

"So the doctor said," she replied serenely.

119

"You go against his express orders." He couldn't keep the rasp of irritation from his tone.

"Shh. Look how sweet Simon is sound asleep," she said in wonderment, her fingers brushing the curly locks back from Simon's brow. She was disobeying Lionel's orders, but with a tender pathos that stirred his jaded heart.

He hardened that heart. "I'm ordering you to leave."

"I'm asking leave to stay."

Her quiet determination bit into his resolve. He was tempted to yield.

But he thought of Simon's awful screams, and Fotherington's conviction that his regimen would save his son.

What did Sophie know? Or he himself?

"You are the tutor. I am the father, and your employer. Put him to bed, pick up the light, and go to your room, Miss Bowerbank."

Her green eyes darkened in defiance, but she tucked Simon into bed with gentle, competent hands.

In the gallery, holding her candles high, she turned on Lionel with sudden fierceness. "I will visit him at night, my lord, and sing him to sleep whenever he asks. And I will fight you on the cold baths. They are cruel."

He wanted to bless her and berate her. He wanted to bestow kisses on her mutinous mouth.

He saw her to her bedroom door, his arms rigid at his side to protect her from himself.

She paused and looked up, a reluctant recruit in Wraxham household politics, he thought ironically, and a brave one.

"My students invite you to a demonstration of the siege of Troy tomorrow morning, my lord. I expect to see you there. If we do not meet in Simon's room later on tonight."

He bowed a slight acknowledgment, and walked away from his sons' new advocate, his unexpected adversary.

Chapter Eleven

And many times the Sons and Daughters too,
Act just the same they see their Father do:
And therefore if they chance to go astray,
The Father pointed out the crooked way . . .
                    —The Answer to the Fifteen Comforts
                              of Matrimony (1706?)

Lionel stood outside the schoolroom door, edgy as an officer on the eve of battle. He flipped open his watch fob to check the time. The delicate golden minute hand ticked relentlessly up to eight o'clock, the early hour Sophie had appointed him to attend the siege of Troy.

There were some things a man in his position was ill advised to do: tell a wife about a mistress, stake his estate on a single hand at cards, and try to be a better father to his sons.

Their troubles proved him a failure at that last. And he had no idea what to expect of ancient Greek history as taught by Sophie Bowerbank and staged by Max, Alex, and Simon Westfall, the sons he'd failed so miserably so far.

He could more profitably spend the morning doing accounts with the unctuous Barnaby Tims, or testing weights and measures in the granary with the arrogant Carter, or reviewing local statutes in preparation for his weekly sitting as magistrate this afternoon.

All were manly and suitable, if tedious, duties attendant upon his new estate, and none of them smacked of kowtowing to his sons' intrepid, interfering tutor.

Who had looked positively edible by candlelight last night, still in her worn blue silk at well past midnight, an image of maternal care, domestic comforts, and ripe womanhood.

Damn, damn, damn. Surely as epic an event as the siege of Troy would take his mind off Sophie. He put away his watch and pushed open the schoolroom door.

Four pairs of anxious eyes looked up, and Lionel stopped in the doorway. He'd never been summoned to a performance of any kind by any of his sons. His father had not once darkened the door of his nursery or his schoolroom. So he hadn't the foggiest notion of what a father did for a command schoolroom performance.

Three lads stood at attention and sounded off as if rehearsed. "Good morning, Father." "Father." "Sir."

Of course they were rehearsed. Sophie Bowerbank, tutoress extraordinaire, had seen to it that they would treat him with respect. But she couldn't make them welcome him, let alone trust him.

"Good morning, sons," he acknowledged.

"Can you stay to see the siege, Father?" Max asked with careful courtesy.

"Come, Father, and let us show you what we built," Alex suggested. But after last night's grilling he was on his guard.

So the next maneuver to end the family wars was up to Lionel. He strode over and knelt by a table that looked as if it had been commissioned from belowstairs. Atop it sprawled an imposing walled city made of dark brown mud. Barracks, huts, and larger buildings fanned out around a square. Surrounding them, toy soldiers that had belonged to Lionel and his brothers stood guard on wide walls. Lionel duly inspected the array, then whistled low to show his appreciation.

Relieved, the twins relaxed.

"Come, see, Father, this was the hardest part." Max took him by the hand and pulled him closer, pointing to the tallest watchtower rising from a wall.

"It fell down twice," Alex explained. "I designed the gates. Miss Bowerbank made us rebuild them to make way for Simon's secret."

"Over here, Papa," Simon said, braving a wobbly invitation.

Lionel's heart pinched. Simon led him to a desk behind a screen and presented him with a four-legged clay-and-stick figure of a . . . What the devil was it? A pregnant pig? Or perhaps a rhinoceros? But it lacked a horn or corkscrew tail.

He squinted, trying for an overall impression. Ah, of course, the fabled Trojan horse, he could see it now. A triumph of seven-year-old design, aided no doubt by his helpful tutor.

Lionel laid an awkward hand on his youngest son's thin shoulder. "That's a fine mount, son," he offered.

Simon's face screwed up with worry, and he whispered, "It's not a real mount, sir, it's a decoy. Like your wooden ducks when you go shooting, Miss Bowerbank says, only for land, not water."

"Ah, yes, so I see," Lionel whispered back. He made a show of leaning over to verify that it was in fact a decoy.

"Troje has a trapdoor where the soldiers hide. But don't tell Max or Alex." Still whispering.

"They don't know?"

"Not where I put it, they don't."

Lionel studied the horse's sides and front and back. "Neither do I," he said, for there was no door in sight.

Simon glanced over his shoulder at his brothers, busy posing toy soldiers on the walls and in the plaza of the town. "It's here, sir."

Simon furtively moved his hand under the horse's belly,

opened a levered door made of twigs and string, and then quickly stuck it back.

Lionel saw Miss Bowerbank's hand in this simple device too. "Very clever, son. I'd never have guessed."

Simon beamed, more of the normal boy about him than Lionel was used to seeing. Lionel sent Sophie an appreciative glance. Her scrubbed morning face glowed with pride above yet another faded, fraying frock. Not that he had any business noticing how scrubbed her face looked. Or how the plainest of old dresses revealed her womanly wanton curves.

Nevertheless he was pleased. In only how many days of tutoring—ten?—she had taken his rapscallions to heart, all three of them.

"I see some restless soldiers here, Miss Bowerbank, keen for action."

"Max, the story," she said on cue but unsmiling, arguably tense.

Alex hovered over the city, restlessly moving the toy soldiers about while Max recited from memory events leading to the siege. Paris, Helen, and Achilles figured in, but he stuttered over the names and roles of Nestor and Agamemnon.

"Simon, are you ready now?" she coaxed.

From where Lionel was standing, only he could see Simon steady the horse on its wooden platform.

Alex shifted from foot to foot, impatient for his turn.

"Alex, the gate," Sophie ordered.

Alex charged around a corner of the table to the massive wall's south gate. Bump! He stumbled over the table's leg.

"Ye-ouch!" he cried as he fell. An arm grabbed for purchase, tearing down the whole front wall of Troy, and Alex crashed amidst a sickening tumble of dried mud and straw and sticks.

Pale with dismay, Simon peered around the screen, ungainly horse in hand.

Alex crumpled, his hands around one knee, fury on his face. "Bloody stupid table."

Lionel reached for him instinctively, but Sophie got there first.

"Alex!" she cried, half censure, half concern, and sank to the floor beside him. "Are you all right? Let's look at your knee."

"His knee?" Max exploded, and swore an oath he was not supposed to know. "Look at our city." He stomped around the table, taking in the damage. "He ruined our work. Days and days of work."

Any tutor Lionel had ever had would have birched both boys on the spot. For an instant, it seemed to him a proper course.

But Sophie's way held sway. "Maxim," she said firmly, "you help Simon check his horse. I need to make sure Alexander isn't badly hurt."

Alex fought tears of pain and mortification. Sophie rolled up the right leg of his trousers, making cheering sympathetic noises.

Lionel, leaning in to see the damage, felt large and useless. His son's kneecap showed a bright red weal. Lionel winced in sympathy. Banged kneecaps were the very devil.

Sophie poked and prodded around the scrape without provoking actual cries. "Can you walk on that leg?" she asked after a few moments.

Alex gave her a disgusted look that said he would walk on it, or die. He took an angry step, and then another.

"Of course I can walk," he snapped.

Protective anger flared in Lionel. "Say 'Yes, thank you, Miss Bowerbank, I believe I can walk quite well.' "

Alex shot him a stunned glance and repeated the injunction word for word. Then he parked himself in front of the ruined wall, shoulders sunk in misery.

"It will take half the morning to put this right," he moaned.

"Not if the Westfall men gather round and work together," Sophie said, and squeezed his shoulder in commiseration.

"Don't fret, Alex. Accidents happen, even in the best-planned sieges. Max and Simon, let's get started."

Ah, this was his cue, Lionel thought with relief. He could count on Sophie to handle this. He headed for the door.

She sprang to her feet and intercepted him. "Excellent idea, my lord," she began, green eyes scheming. "If you will arrange for water and a basin, then you can help us wet the clay again and restore the wall."

He put on patience like a shield. "Contrary to your notions of what an earl might do at his leisure, Miss Bowerbank, I have appointments pending even as we speak."

The green eyes glared, and she hissed in an undertone, "You wouldn't dare desert them now, my lord."

He'd just meant to get out of the way. She did have a point, especially if he hoped to forge bonds of trust with his sons. Still, a man of his standing in the world neither apologized nor explained. "Water, eh. Very well then."

For the first time that morning she bestowed a smile on him, a little arch, a lot engaging. Was she flirting? No, not now, not here, she wouldn't flirt with him.

"It isn't as though I'm asking you to go dig up fresh clay," she said, crossing her arms under her ample bosom.

He felt a lift of arousal but gritted his teeth and forced his thoughts to mud and boyish insurrections.

"I can do that," he growled.

"Good. They need your help, my lord."

Could it be that simple? He played with the notion like a fresh-dealt hand at cards. Could working together bring them closer? Could it make amends for his ill-considered rant last night? Could it even dispel poor Alex's pain?

Approval glinted in a pair of bright green eyes.

Approval, not flirtation.

He had a chance.

He went to fetch a pail of water for his sons with a lighter step than he had taken in years.

*　　*　　*

Lionel returned, sloshing water onto his trousers and the rushes on the schoolroom floor. On second thought, he was ill prepared for this. What did he know of boys, or schoolroom sieges? He and his three brothers never played a game that didn't involve wooden guns and writhing death.

Still, as a captain who'd charged his troops up embattled hills, he knew better than to show hesitation.

"More water, sir. Just so," Max directed.

Dutifully he tipped his bucket, and water trickled over the chunks of smashed and broken wall.

"My turn?" Alex asked, eager to right his wrong. He immersed his hands in the mix of clay, straw, sticks, and dirty water, and stirred and squeezed.

"Bah!" he exclaimed moments later in disgust. "This won't do any good. It's dry."

Max tried too, but his young fingers didn't have the strength to break up the chunks and knead the water in.

Interesting, Lionel thought. *How will Sophie handle this?*

She caught his gaze. "My lord," she said sweetly.

"Yes, Miss Bowerbank?"

What next? He'd brought enough water to float a boat.

She nodded at the muck. *Your turn.*

He scowled back, incredulous. It was his sons' schoolroom, his sons' *task*. He was an invited observer, an honored guest.

"We wouldn't want to leave it soaking through the night," she said, more sweetly still, and yet implacable.

She meant for him to do it, the earl of Wraxham, renowned whip, noted rake, celebrated cynic.

With a groan, he shucked his country jacket, rolled up the sleeves of a fine linen shirt, and plunged his hands into the muddying water. It wasn't hard work for a man, not that playing with clay was a man's work. Nor was it unpleasant, not the clumpy, sucking, squishy part, or his sons' rapt attention.

"There," he said at last, and laid a mound of softened clay the size of a Christmas goose on the table with a surprising rush of pride in his accomplishment.

Max and Alex grinned their thanks, and Lionel's heart squeezed with unaccustomed pleasure. Simon pursed his lips together in imitation of Lionel's whistle when he'd first seen the model city. Lionel gave him a half hug, and swallowed against a lump in his throat.

Sophie lifted her shapely white hands in applause. Well. More successfully this time, Lionel pushed back a randy image of where he wanted to direct her touch.

Because something special, something unexpected, was happening in the bosom of his family.

He and his sons could work together. Perhaps he could do more. He knew military fortifications. He knew how to build a sturdier wall, and he set about helping design it.

He was so deep into an explanation of the most desirable proportions of base to top that he barely noticed when alien footsteps tapped across the schoolroom floor.

"It's Owen Hill, the butcher, my lord, to see you," Lionel's secretary, Barnaby Tims, confided softly.

Probably a billing matter, Lionel thought. Utter nonsense for the man to interrupt him here for that.

"Later, Tims," he all but growled.

"Begging your pardon, my lord, but he says it's urgent."

Billing wasn't urgent, not in a village like Wraxham. Something for the magistrate then. But the magistrate was busy being a father to his sons. Hill could damned well approach the magistrate like everyone else.

"Tell him to bring the matter to Upton Grange this afternoon." He showed the boys how to fix a twig, a supporting member, into the base of the wall before looking up.

The spineless Tims wrung his hands. "It's more urgent than that, my lord, if you would just step outside a moment."

"Can you not see that we are busy here?" he ground out, exasperated.

Simon quailed, Max and Alex stiffened, and Sophie's eyes widened.

Bugger all. He craned his neck at Tims and said more

mildly, "Bring the man here, then, if you must."

The man was here, lurking outside the schoolroom door. The instant Tims opened the door, the butcher stomped in.

"What are you going to do about my carcasses, milord, that's wha' I'd like to know."

Lionel got up, glad he stood a head above the irate, red-faced man. Dried blood stained his heavy muslin apron, but the blood on his hands seemed fresh, and the cleaver on a belt around his waist looked razor-sharp and deadly.

"What do I have to do with your carcasses, Hill?" he asked smoothly, rinsing his hands as he assessed the man. Was such impudence from a villager the upshot of the old earl's misrule?

Hill's head jerked toward Tims. "You didn't tell 'Is Lordship? Bloody 'ell."

Sophie stepped forward. "There are children in this room, Mr. Hill. You can take this dispute and that filthy language outside."

"I'm not taking anything anywhere, ma'am, not when it's them that done it." He shook a ham-sized fist in the direction of the twins. "Everybody in the village knows about you little hellions. You started by ruining the little old ladies' wash, ladies every man jack of us knows are living on soupbones. Soupbones."

The twins' jaws dropped and dropped some more. Lionel took a stand between them, a protective hand on each boy's shoulder, deciding to hear the man out before jumping to conclusions.

"And then Lady Upton's garden," Hill went on. "The village won't stand for it, milord, no matter who you are, bringing those boys down here with their London ways, with no respect for ordinary folk, nothing but pranks and tomfoolery."

"We don't do tomfoolery," Max muttered.

"We didn't do *anything*," Alex protested.

"Slow down and explain yourself, Hill. What the devil happened?"

"I caught your dogs in my shop—three prime pointers and

a setter—everyone saw the boys out hunting with them late yesterday. Those dogs ruined a week's worth of fresh carcasses, everything save for a few lousy pheasants I had strung up from the rafters."

Lionel narrowed his gaze at the man. "And you're accusing my sons of exactly what?"

"Breaking into my butcher shop and setting your dogs loose. For the pure spite o' it," Hill spat out.

There was no spite in his twins, Lionel thought. Their sturdy shoulders stiffened beneath his hands, and he squeezed them in support.

"My dogs, Hill. You're sure about that."

"Primus, my lord," Tims chimed in helpfully. "Drake, Trey, and Willy. Grimsby identified them straightaway and brought them home." Grimsby ran the Wraxham kennels, home to over a hundred foxhounds, pointers, setters, spaniels, and Lionel's new favorite, a lurcher from his Scottish properties near James and Marcus's school.

But how in hell did the dogs get out? His sons didn't do things like that. But he had to question them, in private, though. Not before this enraged slaughterer of lambs and calves and poultry. "I'll talk to them, Hill. But you're going to need proof to bring charges against my sons or anyone else. In my home or in my court."

A bright vein of anger pulsed down the center of Hill's forehead. "I don't need proof, milord. I want punishment. And payment. That was twenty guineas' worth of meat."

"Someone will be punished, Hill, and someone will pay. But not without solid proof. Tims, show Mr. Hill out."

Owen Hill stomped out as he'd stomped in, cleaver swinging from his belt, Tims sulking behind.

Admissions and denials tumbled out of the twins.

Yes, they'd walked the dogs out to the orchard, flushed a pheasant hen and three pigeons, which they weren't allowed to shoot, harassed a grouchy goose and her six goslings nesting by the millpond, skipped stones across the water, and then returned the dogs to Mr. Grimsby.

But no, they hadn't seen the dogs since then, had never stepped foot in Mr. Hill's old smelly butcher shop, had no idea he kept it locked at night, and wouldn't know how to pick a lock to save their lives, although learning that skill seemed a jolly good trick to them.

Instead, they'd slept in their beds through the night, and they were bloody well sorry they'd done so because if they'd been up and about like the men they really, really wished they were, they'd have liked to run down that culprit themselves and truss him up and bring him in to justice.

"Don't you even think of trying to catch that villain," Lionel roared, horrified at the thought.

They quailed, and he repented of his tone, but did not retract his warning. "Someone out there is dangerous, and getting more dangerous by the day."

Max's golden eyes glinted with interest. "How dangerous, sir? Bad enough to hang him?"

"Or to draw and quarter him? We should quite like to see that!" Alex said, greedy for some gore.

Soberly Lionel knelt before them, eye to eye. "Sons, these are serious charges, and we must face them squarely."

"But we didn't do it, Father," said Max, his face strained with earnest disavowal. "We honestly didn't."

"We're already paying for what we did to those old ladies' sheets," Alex added petulantly.

"The Misses Gatewoods' sheets," Sophie corrected. "Anything less is disrespectful, especially coming from you."

"And you're both in enough trouble without adding disrespect and impertinence to your list of proven crimes, which include, by the way, crimes committed in this very room. Have you made your proper apologies to Miss Bowerbank?"

Sophie's brow lifted in surprise.

Max and Alex, perhaps growing used to discipline, squared

their shoulders, precise as soldiers on review, and presented themselves to her before the wreck of Troy.

Lionel suppressed a grin of satisfaction laced with unexpected pride. He liked it that the sons of his loins had spirit. He was beginning to like having a wholesome influence over them. He could only hope he wasn't too late to make a difference in the lives of Graeme, James, and Marcus.

"We apologize, Miss Bowerbank, about the chalk . . ."

". . . and the books and the tables . . ."

". . . and your shawl that day."

They hadn't confessed that one to him, the little blighters.

"And we'll try not to get into trouble anymore."

"Try, gentlemen?" she said, her hands on her hips in challenge.

"Yes, Miss Bowerbank, we'll try very hard," Alex said.

Max elbowed him. "We're supposed to say we'll stop doing things like that altogether, you dolt."

Alex's face twisted, and he whispered to his twin.

The corners of Max's mouth pulled down in disgust. "No matter how clever it is, is what I think they mean."

Alex groaned a heavy "Oh" of disappointment.

Sophie stepped into the silence. "I don't suppose you gentlemen could turn your considerable talents back to the rebuilding of Troy. Your father had the clay just right, and he's still here to help."

He hadn't meant to help beyond mixing the clay, but he wasn't going to desert them after Hill's tirade.

The wall was nearly done, the gate set in place, and mud pretty evenly distributed on the hands and shirts of the father and his sons, when Tims slunk back in with another guest.

Squire Upton wore his grimmest magisterial scowl. He held out a fisted hand and opened it, palm up.

He had marbles, half a dozen winking agate spheres.

"Hey!" Alex stepped up boldly. "Those are ours."

The squire's scowl deepened. "Caught you, you little blackguard."

Max looked from his brother to the marbles and back, their danger dawning.

"What are you doing with our marbles? Sir," he managed to add.

Pity flashed across the squire's face, and then his gaze turned to stone. "With respect, my lord, Roscoe found these this morning ground into the dirt beneath a jumble of branches."

"We never took our marbles to the garden," Alex blurted.

"We were never *in* the garden," Max corrected him.

Lionel's stomach clenched with doubt, and he said in a dead-even voice, "You'd best get your stories straight, sons, if you're going to embark on a life of crime."

Sophie, on the other side of Troy, pulled little Simon closer to her. Even from halfway across the room, Lionel could see her eyes glisten with sympathetic tears. She looked beautiful to him, sensual and womanly, but it touched him most to see that she cared.

He wished *he* didn't have to care, but he cared so much it hurt. Whom did he believe? His adult neighbor, the magistrate? Or his sons, already caught and convicted of stoning those blasted sheets? His heart said believe the boys, but they'd bumbled their explanation of the marbles.

"Do either of you have an idea how the marbles got there?"

Max shuffled. "It wasn't us."

Alex shrugged. "No, sir."

The squire pursed his lips and sadly shook his head.

"If you will step outside, sir," Lionel said, "I will join you in a moment."

Upton left, but Tims lingered. "You too, Tims," Lionel ordered. "This is a family matter." Tims departed, nose clearly out of joint, which was the least of Lionel's problems.

The greatest was his wayward sons, and he was damned if he knew how to tell them that he wasn't letting them out of Wraxham House in his lifetime. Except of course as his neighbors' complaints, his duties as a magistrate, and his responsibilities as their father would compel him to release them to work off their sins in Squire Upton's garden and Owen Hill's butcher shop.

Chapter Twelve

But Man, said I, *I've heard my Mother say,*
Is False, and cannot love above a Day;
Will Swear ten thousand Lyes, to be Believ'd'
And Fawn, *and* Flatter, *tell h'has one Deceiv'd:*
But when h'has gain'd his End, inclin'd to Rove,
Slights what he Vow'd he could for Ages Love.
     —The Answer to the Fifteen Comforts
                of Matrimony (1706?)

Sophie watched Lionel on tenterhooks. He'd prowled to the schoolroom window and stood gazing out on Wraxham's fields, mulling, she imagined, over what to do with Max and Alex. Between their protests of innocence and his doubts about it, her noble plan of patching up matters between them would be ever so much harder now.

Everything would be harder now.

He pushed away from the window and halted before her and his sons with a military click. "A moment with you, Miss Bowerbank, in private if you will."

His steely eyes cut to the door, directing her to the hallway outside. So she set the boys to declining Latin nouns and joined their father, astonished that he was ordering her about, as if he'd forgotten their steamy embrace in the kissing gate.

She hadn't forgotten. How could she, when he stood before her, a tantalizing dusting of dark hair showing in the slash of his open shirt, and his rolled-up sleeves revealing strong corded wrists and forearms—which she'd never seen? Capable of bearing arms, of beating back the enemy, of killing.

"I must apologize, Sophie," he began, closing the schoolroom door behind them, "for involving you in this tangle."

Tangle. He meant *embarrassment*, but she saw another kind of tangle, arms wrapped around each other, legs entwined, tongues probing, seeking. "I—it wasn't your fault, my lord," she stammered. "You couldn't have predicted it would come to this."

"If I had guessed it, I never would have enlisted you to teach the scoundrels."

She scowled. "You cannot think them guilty, my lord."

"Of anything they confess to, yes. As to the rest," he said, grating out the words with evident frustration, "a magistrate cannot accept their pleas of innocence."

"I think they are sincere, my lord. And they apologized to me so sweetly."

"The marbles were theirs," he said grimly. "Alex recognized them."

She had recognized them. The boys always had their marbles on hand, and played behind her back, but she wasn't about to add that damning evidence to Lionel's present wrath.

"All boys have marbles," she said in their defense.

"Of course, someone could have planted them afterward to implicate them," he said gravely. "Perhaps even you."

"I wouldn't have, my lord, never," she blurted, aghast.

A ghost of a smile twisted his mouth.

"You shouldn't tease about such treachery," she added.

"So I can rest assured that their esteemed tutor, the rector's

136

daughter, did not plant the marbles. Never mind that the boys have plagued her schoolroom with their pranks and invaded her boudoir."

"Boys' pranks, my lord. An excess of energy and imagination."

"So how did the marbles get to the garden, if they were not lost while the boys were in the act? Vandals, Gypsies? As well to wonder about Tims or Carter. And we might as well throw in Beane, who skulks around, or Laframboise, who hasn't had a good word for Wraxham House since I moved him to the country."

"If you are speculating that wildly, my lord, why not throw in Mrs. Plumridge, who no longer rules the roost with your father gone? And Nurse Nesbit resents my very breath," Sophie said, hoping to evoke a smile.

But Lionel strode off, thinking, then came back to the question of the boys. "Damnation. They thought it a lark. We would have in their shoes, my brothers and I."

"I refuse to believe they did it," Sophie said.

"Bloody hell, Sophie. I'm their father, and I don't want to believe it. But as magistrate, I must investigate their guilt. The more so since the business of the dogs."

"But the dogs could have been . . ." She didn't quite know what.

That twist of a smile again. "You didn't release the dogs as well?"

She scowled. "Not funny, my lord."

"I thought not. I can't think of a soul who would do such a thing."

Sophie felt his anger gaining ground, her arguments losing it. But she stood up to him. "You must see that the dogs simply could have gotten loose."

"The exact same four dogs they'd taken out that afternoon?" He clenched his jaw, his thoughts clearly taking a darker turn. "Not bloody likely."

She saw his point, and worse yet, sympathized with his position. "What are we going to do, my lord?"

An odd expression flicked across his face, but he masked it. "You are to go forward as you have begun, with lessons all morning long. Make them rigorous, demanding lessons. Make the boys work."

With that directive, her last efforts to smooth his way with his sons collapsed. "I refuse to punish them for crimes they may not have committed."

"It's not punishment, not yet. It's control. Don't leave them a single minute free to dream up another crime. And no more amusing games with model villages and toy soldiers."

Her spirit flared in their defense. "But they worked so well together, my lord, and with such enthusiasm."

"Let them develop enthusiasm for facts and sums."

"It's not the right way, my lord," she cautioned.

He brushed off her warning. "They can practice working together in the afternoons with Squire Upton's gardener."

She crossed her arms in disapproval. "Considering your present mood, it's a good thing they found no marbles at the butcher's."

"They found the dogs, and that's enough."

"Surely you're not going to punish the boys over a completely unconfirmed accusation."

He gave her a repressive look. "No, but I am going to buy Hill's shop full of ruined carcasses, and feed them at the kennels."

"You cannot do that," she blurted, dropping the form and courtesy she owed to Lionel's position, if to nothing else.

He arched a brow in warning. The scar that angled across it was white. "I cannot, Miss Bowerbank?"

She would not let him intimidate her, not with his maleness or his class. "Buying Hill's stock would be tantamount to admitting they did it."

Anger tightened his mouth. "Some may see it that way."

"But they didn't do it," she persisted.

"Didn't they? Think, Sophie. Past experience suggests otherwise. Present appearances are damning. These are not small crimes, but malicious mayhem, and my neighbors, my tenants—who have lived here for generations—are upset. No one has reason to fabricate these accusations."

"What are you saying? Boys lie, but their elders don't?"

He groaned, but continued, "I am saying that boys don't know the value of things. I was one once. Boys don't see the consequences of adventures. Boys make mistakes."

"And therefore they are guilty," she said.

"Therefore, I will make amends. They will make amends."

His temper and his pride had overcome him. "I warn you, my lord. This will not win their hearts."

"I will do what I must to protect my sons, to protect them from themselves. Can I assume your support, Miss Bowerbank?"

"Yes, my lord. I will stay with your boys," she said, her own temper kicking in. "Someone needs to protect them from your wrath."

His face shuttered. "Just keep them busy, Miss Bowerbank," he ordered and struck off down the gallery.

Sophie gasped. And not only at the force of his final order.

For behind the void where he had towered over her stood Celia, her blue eyes flashing. She rushed up and clasped Sophie's arms below the puffed sleeves that capped her shoulders.

"Oh, Sophie, you poor thing. Men are such beasts," she said in a sympathetic hiss.

Lionel a beast? She had thought him lionlike, fierce in the management of his young, and angry and perplexed. But not a beast, never—then it struck her: "You *listened* to my conversation with Lord Wraxham."

Celia drew herself up. "I am your chaperone. Would you have preferred for me to interrupt?"

"I should have preferred for you to turn away."

Celia looked hurt. "I was afraid for you. As your companion, I am here to—"

"To eavesdrop?"

She slipped a conciliatory hand in Sophie's. "I came on you quite by chance, and I'm so glad I did. Pray, don't be angry, dearest. I am on your side."

Sophie wasn't angry. She was appalled and offended, and she felt exposed that anyone had overheard her very private argument with Lionel where she had gone so far past cheeky and insubordinate that she'd sounded almost like a wife. A fishwife.

"I never would have thought His Lordship could be such a bully," Celia went on.

"Lord Wraxham, a bully?" Sophie said. "A desperate father, perhaps, at his wits' end."

Celia's mouth primmed. "That's not how I saw it."

"What did you see? No, more to the point, just how much did you hear?"

"Enough to know he's put you in a terrible position. It is so unfair of him to make you the instrument for punishing those boys."

Sophie had felt that herself, but how unfair had he been? So many signs pointed particularly to them, and no other plausible suspects had stepped to the stage of their little drama. "Lord Wraxham has to take everything into account, even the marbles and the dogs."

"Marbles? Dogs?" Celia scowled in pretty confusion. "Good Lord, Sophie, what more can they have done?"

Sophie bit her lower lip, vexed to have let so much slip out and determined to say no more.

"I can be of no use to you if you keep me in the dark," Celia pointed out.

Reluctantly Sophie summarized the morning's revelations.

Celia listened gravely. "This is ever so much worse than I imagined."

"Promise to keep it to yourself," Sophie said.

"You must promise to be careful. I'm afraid it's time to get you out of here. You may not be safe," Celia warned.

But Celia was terrified of harmless garden snakes. "Don't worry," Sophie said. "At the first sign of danger, I shall call on you."

"You do that, dearest. You can depend on me."

Sophie wasn't sure whom she could depend on anymore. Lionel's sons were a trial, Lionel was a puzzle, and she was in over her head.

But they needed her, each and every one of them. She would spurn her oldest friend's gently tendered advice before she would desert Lionel and his sons.

Sophie hastily dressed for dinner in an old yellow muslin frock. It made her look almost as weary as she felt. But she deemed it respectable enough for a lowly tutor charged to do nothing more than follow orders.

Downstairs, the Wraxham ship of state was launching. Mrs. Plumridge sailed toward the mammoth sideboard like the prow of a mighty merchantman. An armada of lesser vessels—valiant footmen—trailed her with tureens of soup, platters of game, and covered dishes of vegetables.

"In England, Monsieur Laframboise," she was saying, "we begin our meals with hearty soups, not rabbit food."

Monsieur Laframboise, the stolen chef, puffed his fiery red cheeks. "Zee zoup first, eet ees—*comment dites vous?*—an abominable?"

"The word, monsieur, is *abomination.* If you have truly lived in England fifteen years, you might at least try not to butcher our language."

"Baugh, madame! Next you weel tell me to follow zee recipes of zee chefs *l'Anglais.* And zat I weel not do. I have my pride, and my standards."

Sophie had standards of her own, and they were being tested. The twins arrived and started fencing with their dinner knives, parry, thrust, and kill.

"For heaven's sake," she scolded as she stripped them of their heavy silver cutlery. "You lot are in trouble enough."

"But, Miss Bowerbank, we worked all afternoon—"

"—in Lady Upton's garden."

She narrowed her eyes. "Let me see your hands." They stuck out their square, sturdy hands. "They're clean," she said, suspicion mounting. "Too clean."

They shared a glance. "We are embarked on a course of reform, Miss Bowerbank," said Max, soberly aping the very lecture she had given in the schoolroom after their father left.

"Which includes clean hands, ma'am," added Alex docilely. But mischief gleamed in his brown eyes.

Ha! They'd either actually washed their hands or never stepped foot inside that garden. She could test that handily enough. "Lady Upton's gardener's name is . . ."

"Mr. Eliot," he said promptly. Correctly.

"And what tasks did Mr. Eliot assign you this afternoon?"

"We dug holes, deep holes, wide holes. He said we weren't half bad for horrid little hellions," Max said proudly.

"Hellions?" she mused. There was something to it. If not full-blown, they were hellions in the making.

Alex grinned. "I asked if it meant that we were going to hell."

"What was his answer?"

"He reckoned the devil would be doubly pleased with twins."

So that was the source of that mischievous glint, she thought, pressing her lips against a smile. They were good-natured boys to find fun in punishment. She wished Lionel had overheard their innocent devilment, so like his and his brothers' reputation as boys. It might soften him.

She handed them their dinner knives. "These are your own knives, I presume."

"Yes."

"Then put them back at your places, and go wait for your father. I'm sure he will be along in a moment."

They bounded to the table, obviously pleased with themselves. She said a little prayer that she had struck the right mix of discipline and lenience.

But where was their father? Where was Simon?

For that matter, where was Celia?

Just then, the dining room doors swung open, and Celia entered, pink with distress, clinging to Lionel's arm.

Under his other arm was Simon, flushed with anger.

"Miss Bowerbank, be so kind as to take your charge"—Lionel glanced down at his captive son—"and his snake back to the nursery."

Simon's new snake curled in and out about his fingers, a pale green garden creature, no longer than the boy's forearm, with a bright yellow throat and dark blotches along its sides.

Celia shrank from it in horror. "If you could just get rid of that writhing serpent, my lord," she begged, her breathy whisper tremulous.

Sophie hurried over. "Wait, wait! I'll take them both."

"Don't hurt my snake," Simon cried as his father passed him off to Sophie. To her satisfaction, her ploy of a pet snake was helping Simon overcome his fear of snakes in dreams. He quite liked live snakes in daylight and had fast befriended his own personal serpent.

"We'll just go up to your room," Sophie said in the most calming voice that she could manage.

"Oh no!" Celia cried. Her perfectly proportioned bosom heaved with distress in the very line of Lionel's sight. "Don't you dare take that snake upstairs. I could not have a moment's peace, knowing there was a reptile in the house."

Lionel looked down at Celia with something Sophie hoped was just compassion, and then glared up at her. "I understand that this was Miss Bowerbank's idea. She will take care of the snake."

But not kill it, Sophie vowed. Fortunately, Lionel had not ordered execution.

"Come, Simon," she said. "Let's go see Nurse Nesbit."

*　　*　　*

It took Sophie a quarter hour to calm the lad and return his snake to a safe haven. She had to demonstrate that it was perfectly secure in its jar with ants to eat, grass to curl about in, and holes punched in the lid for air.

"But you can keep it," she assured him. "Miss Upton never comes to your quarters, so she won't be the wiser . . . so long as you promise not to tell and never, ever show it off to her again."

Simon promised vehemently, and she led him back downstairs. He calmed with talk of safer subjects, and Sophie congratulated herself on averting a disaster. Soon their footsteps echoed off the black-and-white-marbled floors of Wraxham's grand front entrance. Footman Thomas Beane was opening the door to admit a tall, lean stranger. The man's fashionable attire, though rumpled, showed him to be well placed.

Yet even from behind, Sophie saw tension, if not outright hostility, in his dishevelment.

"Welcome home, my lord," Beane said cautiously.

Simon bolted for the man. "Graeme!" he yelped in delight.

Sophie gawked. Graeme? Graeme Westfall, Lord Cordrey? Lionel's heir, and Simon's oldest brother.

Wasn't he supposed to be at the university?

Lord Cordrey, Lionel's hope and Wraxham's future, slapped a smart beaver hat, ebony cane, and immaculate kid gloves into the footman's waiting hands, and scooped Simon in his arms.

"What ho, tadpole? Who let you out?" he teased, but his tone seemed forced.

Sophie hung back, unwilling to intrude.

"I'm not a tadpole!"

"How very odd. You were last time I saw you. Never say you've turned into a frog."

"Nooo," Simon wailed with glee. "I should like to be a prince."

"That's more like it." Cordrey tousled his little brother's chestnut hair, then over the top of his head, said starkly,

"Where's my father, Beane? Dining, I should think."

"Yes, my lord, they're in the dining room."

"Best to get this over with," Graeme muttered, mounting a joyfully wriggling Simon atop his shoulders.

"Very good, sir. They will not have started yet, not without these two." Beane indicated Sophie with a nod.

Graeme turned to see her, and Sophie stifled a shock of recognition. Graeme was the spitting image of the nineteen-year-old Lionel she'd loved, tall, tawny, beautiful, and brooding.

Graeme scowled in suspicion, his sharp gaze noting her worn dress and unfashionable hair.

He gave a perfunctory bow. "Should I know you, madam?"

"She's Miss Bowerbank," Simon chirped with pride.

She smiled and gave a hasty curtsey. "Tutor to your younger brothers, my lord."

"Now here's a new twist for Father," the new viscount snorted in disbelief.

Oh dear, he must think Lionel was keeping a mistress under the guise of tutor, understandable in light of his father's reputation. Which simply was not the case, in spite of her bawdy imaginings. What a setback for her campaign to reunite Lionel with his sons, with this particular son.

So she carefully spoke as tutor. "I am sure the twins will be as pleased to see you as Simon. You are just in time for dinner. Will you join the boys and me? Your little brother would be over the moon."

He lofted Simon up again and walked along beside her, a dark cloud of . . . she could not tell what. Perhaps he held her in contempt, but his misery seemed to be his own. What could be the matter?

Young lords had great freedom to come and go, but this young lord's arrival was unannounced and out of season. Nor could he know the family chaos he was walking into.

She could only pray he wasn't about to add to it.

Chapter Thirteen

Above a Year or two I always thought
My Wife so good that she cou'd not be naught,
Till one Night coming home I caught a Spark
Sat in my Parlor by her in the dark . . .
My am'rous Wife's Gallant, before he went,
Did shew enough t' encrease my Discontent
For he wou'd slily pull her Petticoat,
Nod, Wink, and put into her Hand a Note,
Whisper her in the Ear, or touch her Foot
With many other private Signs to boot . . .
—The Fifteen Comforts of Cuckoldom (1706)

Another narrow escape, Lionel thought, after Sophie left with Simon.

But he couldn't help his attraction to her. He liked Sophie best in faded muslins, whether gray or green or rose made no difference as long as they looked soft and draped her figure to hint at her tempting curves.

Her simple muslin dresses took him back to their old haunts

and habits, back to his youthful obsession with everything about her, her face lit up over a line of poetry, her flesh firm beneath the muslin's softness, her skin dewy when he untied her laces and revealed it. Those dresses spoke to him of bookish earnestness and country passion.

Of waywardness and dalliance and desire. On a mossy riverbank, in the afternoon, he remembered the pillowy plumpness of her bared breasts, the tremor of pure lust in his eager hands.

Celia he would gladly deposit in the tony London salons she clearly aspired to. Her manners were exquisite and her conversation was fastidious, but she made him think of drawing room rules and dance floor rituals, of the calculated kisses of his marriage bed. So near, so tremblingly alive, Celia had all but drowned him in refined sensibilities and an attar of rare roses. She marched right along with a parade of grasping London ladies he had once taken or tossed off as he pleased.

Simon's snake had given Lionel the measure of the two mismatched friends. Ever vigilant for his attention, Celia had taken it as an excuse to gain a handhold on his person.

And a bruising grip she had, he thought wryly.

No snakes, horror! Slimy creeping things.

Silly woman, to think he'd fall for that.

Not so Sophie, he thought. She'd grown into so much more than the girl he'd betrayed and left behind, fearless of snakes and men like him. In his years away, his biddable lass had grown sure of who she was. She was determined, intrepid.

Not only had she cleverly introduced the reptile for his son's improvement, she'd stood up to Lionel as father and as earl, unimpressed by title or tradition. Already she'd proven herself a better mother to his sons than their own mother, rational and smart, caring but firm, a woman any decent man would be proud to marry.

A decent man, not him.

His heart was too jaded, his urges too long unsatisfied. With her ever present, he couldn't repress an almost constant state of rut. If he didn't get a handle on his rampaging lust, he'd have to head up to London for a couple of bouts of mindless swiving. His old friend the duchess or the actress Ariadne would oblige him, demanding nothing but their own pleasure, made more erotic because of his reputation and his title.

Truth was, he didn't want to get a handle on his lust. He simply wanted Sophie, refreshing, tempting, unjaded woman that she was. He wanted to take her on the carpet, in the closets, on the stairs, anywhere his sons weren't.

The rake he used to be would compromise her in a heartbeat.

He winced. The lad he used to be had done so.

But the man he aspired to be was fighting base desire.

He'd vowed to change, to be respectable, responsible. For his sons' sake, and now too for the rector's daughter.

A stir outside the dining room skittered across his senses like fingers on his skin.

Sophie had returned with Simon. Dinner, and conversation, could begin.

"Duck your head, tadpole," a male voice ordered.

Lionel tensed. It was Graeme's voice. Simon's boyish laughter echoed down the hall, then Sophie's light tread, mixed with Graeme's heavier footsteps. The twins bounded to the door, vying for their brother's arms and legs, and crying, "Graeme, Graeme! You're home, you're home!"

"We have ponies here!" said Max.

"Wait till you see the fishing pond," Alex added.

"Can we take you riding tomorrow?" Max pled.

Lionel stiffened. Graeme, his eldest son, his heir, had come home to Wraxham House.

In May, in Trinity term, in the middle of the week.

The news could not be good.

But his arrival spelled great good fortune to his younger brothers. Max and Alex besieged him, pummeling him and winding themselves around him.

Graeme had always had the air of a poet about him. Tonight he appeared to be a pale one, a starving dweller of garrets, a dissolute frequenter of wayside inns and sordid bars, subject to the temptations of gaming and low women and the ravaging emotions of that life.

What the devil had happened?

Lionel stepped up to relieve him of his brothers, but Celia Upton hustled over, aglow at the prospect of yet more noble prey.

Graeme lowered Simon into Sophie's arms and took a measure of her chaperone's blond beauty, clad in city finery. Then he gave an exaggerated, not exactly courteous, bow.

"Duchess, I presume. What a pleasure to meet you. At last."

Bloody hell. His son thought Celia was the duchess of Morace, his longtime lover, whom he'd purposely left behind in her natural habitat, the debauchery of London.

How did Graeme know about the duchess?

Sophie evidently hadn't known, but she suspected something now. To his chagrin, her creamy complexion paled, and she lowered her gaze to her tightly clasped hands.

Celia Upton fluttered before his heir. "You flatter me, Lord Cordrey," she said and gave her real name.

But not, Lionel noted, her father's rank or her modest position at Wraxham House.

When he thought it could get no worse, Graeme turned on him, a tremor of outrage playing about his mouth.

"My mother is not nine weeks in her grave, sir. And I come home to find you with not one but two unattached and unaccompanied women."

Max and Alex goggled, and even Simon blinked.

"Oh," Celia Upton gasped in astonished and offended virtue.

Sophie blushed a shocked bright red.

As for Lionel, the insult, the assumption, jolted him, the more so as he had eyes now for only Sophie. Never mind that in his old life with any other two unescorted women, Graeme's assumption might have been true.

So it was extremely gratifying to face his eldest and find himself still taller, still heavier, still able to make him flinch.

"You are out of line, son," he growled in a low, controlled tone for Graeme's ears only. "Take your insolence and your sordid assumptions to the gun room. None of the guns is loaded. I will meet you after I repair the damage you have wrought."

Lionel choked down dinner, lumps of lamb, pieces of plump partridge, warm wine. Repairing the damage caused by Graeme's insults to the ladies would be no easy task. Lionel could not assure his younger sons that their beloved brother would be there in the morning when he didn't know why he was here tonight. He could not satisfy Celia's burning curiosity, nor would he if he could.

And he couldn't take Sophie in his arms and apologize for his son's insolence, for the specter of the duchess, for the excesses of his life as a licentious rake coming home to roost.

He wouldn't stand to see her wronged again, as she had been by their fathers, and by him.

Lionel half listened as the ladies patched up the evening with talk of poetry and plays. He'd come to Wraxham planning to reform, but his well-meant plans were castles in the air until he got results.

Today, despite everything he'd set out to do, he was no better than the man he'd always been, the rake Graeme had known as father. So Graeme's assumption about the women had not been unreasonable. But his choice of time and place and audience couldn't have made Lionel look worse. As a father Lionel had never faced a greater challenge. How to talk to a son who thought him a wastrel, who'd reached manhood without his influence? How to make up for a lifetime lost?

Lionel dragged himself to the gun room. Life would be easier if he hadn't had so many sons. But he couldn't fault himself for marrying Graeme's mother, not with six strong, spirited sons to show from the union. Because he loved this son and each of the others with a fierce lonely pride he'd kept secret for years, almost from himself.

And still the question nagged him: Why was Graeme home?

He'd find out. Resolved, Lionel strode into the gun room, taking in its familiar antlered walls and breathing in its smell of oil and metal. Usually they calmed him. He was a crack shot from his military days, and hunting, unlike life or women, had clear rules and simple goals.

Being a father did not. He had no instincts for it. His own father had treated him no better than a plant, giving him just enough water to stay alive. He'd never meant to treat his sons as his remote, indifferent father had treated him.

A few small logs burned cheerily in the hearth, and he could see Graeme's ash-brown hair above the back of a favorite chair. Himself, younger.

Lionel stopped by the liquor cabinet, poured two single malts, and offered one to Graeme, man to man.

Graeme stood and took it, a defiant look about him. Lionel rankled. Graeme should be mortified that he'd leaped to conclusions and insulted innocent women.

"You must not remember Miss Bowerbank, the rector's daughter," Lionel began evenly, his back to the little fire. "I hired her to tutor your brothers shortly after we came down. Miss Upton, Squire Upton's only daughter and Miss Bowerbank's friend, is here as her companion. So you can see the error of your hasty assumptions."

Graeme squared his shoulders, a promising start. "I see it now, sir. And I apologize."

"You will have to apologize to them—to Miss Bowerbank, that is. Miss Upton seems to have taken your error in stride."

"I will, at the first opportunity," he said, then cleared his throat and swirled his drink. "I'm here on other business, sir. I thought it imperative to arrive before the letter you are about to receive."

"Letter," Lionel repeated, taking a burning swallow of the malt. There was only one reason his son would come home from Oxford in May to tell him of a letter. "You've been sent down from the university."

"Yes, sir." He didn't elaborate.

So. His eldest son had come home afoul of a university known for its indulgence of young peers, and was determined not to make this interview easy.

Every reason for expulsion Lionel had ever heard of pounded through his brain, in order from bad to worst.

"I don't suppose we can hope you failed to complete your studies," he began.

A shadow of a smile flicked across Graeme's face. "I enjoy the work, sir."

"You haven't written one of those atheistic tracts like Mr. Shelley's." Percy Shelley had been sent down only a few years ago for a tract professing his disbelief in God.

"I found it interesting, but not compelling."

Gambling, then. "If you have overextended yourself, I should warn you, funds are scarce."

"No, sir. Gaming doesn't interest me."

Lionel cupped his tumbler in both hands, and shrugged. "The letter will tell if you don't. But I can stand the shock."

Graeme took a fortifying drink, but added nothing.

"Unless you were very enterprising, that leaves only public drunkenness or lewd behavior."

"Not exactly either, sir. You might say I was keeping my transgressions in the family tradition," Graeme finally said, wry but wary, without trust.

Lionel lifted a hand, palm up, and waited for his son's confession.

"My tutor caught me with his wife."

Lionel winced. So that explained the devastated demeanor. Lionel was suddenly sure he'd had that exact same look that summer over Sophie. Sophie, always Sophie. He had been in love. His father had heaped coals of fire on his bruised heart, railing about his disregard of family, about his need to marry money, and then had banished him to the army to ensure a wrenching separation of lover from beloved. He'd fought signing up to the bloody end, when his father gave his ultimatum:

Go, or he'd ruin Bowerbank—and Sophie, to boot.

He would not berate his own son so. A handsome, romantic lad like Graeme had to be at risk from worldly women. And could profit from the guidance of a rake.

"Rotten luck," Lionel said at last, sounding a great deal more disinterested than he felt. "I imagine you were not her first."

Graeme flushed with instant anger. "What do you take her for, sir?"

He gave his son a level look. "I take her for an adulteress, and so will the law. Are there charges?"

Graeme blanched. "I—not yet, sir."

"Expected then?"

"We don't know. He was old and . . ."

"Impotent." Lionel hazarded a hopeful guess. If so, there was almost kindness there, for a vigorous young man to swive a neglected wife.

But Graeme had said *we*.

"Depraved, sir, and she is inno—"

"*Not* innocent," Lionel grated, holding his temper by a thread. "Am I to understand that you set yourself up to rescue another man's wife?"

"In a manner of speaking, yes, sir, I did. She has left him."

Left him? And into whose care? Lionel almost roared, but he remembered his father's purple rage and scurrilous deprecations against Sophie, whose brains and breasts he'd loved with equal passion and sincerity, and reined in his fury. "So there will be expenses. I advise against setting her up as your mistress."

Graeme stiffened. "I have no intention of doing so, sir."

"Good. If she was clever enough to attract a man of learning, we can find her a position as a governess. In Ireland."

"Actually, sir, I plan to marry her."

Lionel flung his whiskey into the fire, crystal crashing, flames leaping, and roared, "Marry! You must be mad."

Graeme set his jaw. "I knew you would say that, sir."

"Of course I said that. But let me make myself more plain.

You cannot marry a married woman. You cannot waltz up to a judge and get her a divorce. You cannot afford, at least not now in the estate's present indebtedness, to marry without a thought to the woman's class and dowry," Lionel said, vexed to hear his father's tone come through despite his determination to do better by his own son. But this was different, wasn't it?

Graeme met his gaze. "The marriage can be annulled. It was never consummated."

"How in the name of all that's holy do you know the marriage was not consummated?"

Graeme's face flamed. "She was intact, sir."

"She was intact"—Lionel masked his dread with steely skepticism—"until you breached her."

Graeme grimaced with the pain of speaking about something plainly private. "I did not breach . . . When I realized that she wasn't, that she hadn't . . . that her passion was pure and I should respect—"

"There is nothing pure about a married woman kissing a man she is not married to," Lionel said, punching the words instead of his gullible son. Damn the conniving shrew. "Nothing to respect."

"You should know, sir," Graeme said.

As an insurrection, it was quietly mounted, but this first volley hit home. Lionel saw a nobility about the dreamy lad that he had never seen, a hint that Graeme could someday take the reins of Wraxham capably, with backbone, possibly with honor.

All the more reason to persuade him of the folly of his plan. "I do know, and that is why I find your story difficult to credit."

Graeme's expression did not change. "I can understand why a man who sleeps with harlots, wives, and widows would not credit that."

Fair enough, Lionel thought. But Graeme's accusations grated on him. How did his son know? And how had he found out? Blast his late, unlamented wife. For Lionel had no doubt

154

that Penelope had told tales. But Lionel said nothing. He would never run her down to Graeme, not even now, not even over this.

"You never loved my mother." Graeme pressed his lips together, then said vehemently, "You probably never loved anybody, not even that girl you abandoned—" He broke off, blanched.

Lionel's blood ran cold. Graeme couldn't know about Sophie too. "That girl I abandoned," he repeated, his voice hard as stone.

"I'm sorry, sir," Graeme said, clearly mortified. "I have no right—"

"Who do you think I abandoned?" he insisted.

"When you were young like me, someone younger, someone here. The girl you were seeing when Grandfather sent you off to war."

He hadn't said her name. He did not know that someone had been Sophie. Lionel relaxed a fraction. "Who told you this?"

"Sir, I couldn't say."

Lionel sighed, shrugged. "I never hid that from your mother." But she'd hid things from him. She would have used this tale to poison his heir against him.

Graeme hovered stubbornly over the desk. "You insulted my mother before you even knew her," he said fiercely. "And now her memory."

"I did, and I regret it." For Lionel regretted everything, the estrangement of his son far more than the mild annoyance of his manipulative wife. "It's not a path I'd advise you to take."

Graeme cut him a hostile look. "Why not? You made a life of it."

"And look where we ended up, you and I."

"No love lost between father and son, you mean?" He gave an unconvincing shrug of indifference. "That is usual among my friends."

"We could go on like this, forever. It was that way between

your grandfather and me," Lionel said evenly, hanging on to his frayed temper.

"Therefore you assumed we didn't need a father," Graeme said, his voice cracked with pain.

Yes, Lionel thought. *Stupid sod,* he berated himself. "I think you need one now."

Graeme retreated under a blank expression. If he needed a father, he clearly didn't want one. "I should like to be excused, sir."

"We will resume tomorrow morning," Lionel told him, turning to the door to leave, "and with fresher—" He broke off.

For Sophie stood there, frozen, wretched.

Lionel's stomach clenched. She could have heard anything. Everything. "Sophie . . ." he began, startled by surprise into using her given name before his son.

Graeme darted him a condemning look.

Sophie stepped up in her bold way, but her face was white. "Forgive me, my lord, for interrupting. Simon's snake has gone missing. Miss Upton is shrieking, and Simon is beside himself. Max and Alex are searching all the rooms."

"I am coming, Miss Bowerbank," he said, correcting his too-familiar use of her given name.

Graeme snorted and moved to leave, but Lionel blocked him, not a subtle or a wise move, but it worked.

"We will resolve this in the morning," Lionel said, the major he had once been resurfacing to pull a raw recruit in line.

Waves of anger poured off his wronged son, but Graeme managed a slight nod of submission and left, storming past Sophie with a barely civil "Good evening, Miss Bowerbank."

Lionel followed his retreat, a sick feeling in his gut. "God, Sophie, I apologize. For both of us. What did you hear?"

She managed a tight smile, and an empathetic green gaze. "Enough to see that you are dealing with a young man in love."

Lionel swore a dark oath. "I mean about yourself. Us."

"I never assumed our secret was safe, or my ruin forgotten. Else I might have married."

"You could have married. You were still—"

"A virgin, my lord?" she asked, her green gaze clear. "I was in fact, perhaps, but not in my heart. I could not give myself as pure to a decent man, knowing what I knew of you."

She hadn't married on a point of honor. She hadn't married because of him. He closed his eyes and saw dark swirling clouds of self-condemnation. Then he looked into her earnest open face. "I can never make this up to you."

She smiled slightly, without the rancor or disgust he so richly deserved. "No, my lord, you cannot. I cannot make it up to myself. But there are worse things than ruin. I live my life, a satisfying life."

Not likely, he thought, at her father's beck and call, and now at his. "If ever I can do anything . . ."

"You can help me find the snake."

They didn't find the snake. He and the twins searched every bedroom along the hallway, dripping candle wax on a dozen of the finest Aubusson carpets in the south of England and scaring up three mice, several dozen moths, and a great deal more dust than Lionel thought Mrs. Plumridge would ever have permitted.

The twins had a ripping good time.

Nesbit was called to administer smelling salts to Celia. Then she stood by Celia's bed pouring her a draught of Lionel's oldest and best brandy to steady her frazzled nerves.

Sophie engaged Simon in a much quieter search of his room, hoping the snake had not gone far and she could calm its owner.

But who would calm *him?* Lionel thought. For his best intentions were going up in smoke and his household was at sixes and sevens and his family's future lay in the hands of a nineteen-year-old in love with another man's wife.

Sophie could. Sophie.

Chapter Fourteen

What Strange tumultuous Joys upon me seize!
My Breasts do heave, and languish do my Eyes,
Panting's my Heart, and trembling are my Thighs;
I sigh, I wish, I pray and seem to die,
In one continu'd Fit of Ecstacy . . .
  —The Fifteen Plagues of a Maiden-Head (1707)

How to calm herself. The bawdy book she'd purloined from
Lionel's library only proved how frustrated and distracted she
was. She'd never enjoyed the scandalous tales of cloistered
nuns, but she usually took pleasure in the married lady's advice to a maid.

Not tonight. Its graphic description of a wedding night only
made her wonder about the private parts of Lionel's anatomy
with its *darts* and *arrows* and *members*, and other words so
lewd they left out most of the letters.

Sophie sat up in bed, and tucked the book under her pillow.
What a day she'd had, a day filled with Lionel at every crisis.
Lionel with his sleeves rolled up after the botched siege of

Troy. Lionel scolding her about Simon's snake. Lionel defending her to his son down in the gun room. She'd eavesdropped on most of their conversation, unwilling to interrupt, transfixed by all the revelations.

Blast! She was turning into Celia. Sophie snuffed her candle and watched moonlight fill the room, dangling her feet off the enormous four-poster bed in her wine-dark chamber.

She'd gotten what all eavesdroppers deserved, her come-uppance. The young Lord Cordrey, Londoner and Oxonian, hadn't recognized her, but knew his father had ruined someone. So much for reputation. And Celia's presence here at Wraxham House was only window dressing.

Sophie drew her heavy dressing gown around her simple night rail, but its woolen folds felt oh, so hot on the mild May evening. The day had thrown her together with Lionel far more than her overwrought imagination could manage.

She was drawn to him inexorably, inescapably. It wasn't just his physical stature, although his nearness sent her stomach into coils of hot recognition. It wasn't the military side of him, first seen in the siege of Troy, although he'd been both expert and kind in showing his sons how to rebuild that wall. It wasn't the experienced rake, although his advice to his son stirred steamy fantasies about Lionel as a London rake.

No, she still cared for him, most of all when he was most put out. The ups and downs of his life were fast becoming the ups and downs of hers.

So were Simon's. She huddled her old dressing gown around her. After failing to find the dratted snake, she'd read to Simon and tucked him into bed, ignoring Dr. Fotherington's injunction to leave him to himself.

But she worried for the little tyke. If she'd found the day chaotic, he must be reeling from it. She couldn't be certain he was resting peacefully, and she wanted to be there if he was not.

She tugged the belt of her dressing gown tight. It would be awkward to encounter Lionel when she was in a state of near undress. Awkward, but interesting. Her breath hitched in anticipation. Should she even take a candle? No. Moonlight shining through the great tall hallway windows would show her way.

She cracked open her door, looking up and down the vast vaulted hallway. The venerable old mansion breathed with the spirits of august ancestors. But there was no activity—no pans rattled from the kitchen, no servants walked overhead, no clothing whispered, no servants padded past, or vagrant boys, or men. Even the mice they'd stirred up hunting for Simon's snake had tunneled back into their nests.

She tiptoed along the carpeted hall, barefoot for stealth, counting: two doors, three doors, five.

How liberating, how lonely, to roam Wraxham's storied halls while Lionel lay safely sleeping in a bed she'd never seen, would never see.

The moon slid behind a bank of clouds, and she touched her fingers to the wall to keep her bearings. She did not need candles, or moonlight. The sixth door. Next would be the twins' and then Simon's—

Her shin jammed into a loglike barrier, her bare toes tangled in the carpet, her arms pinwheeled in the air, and she was falling . . . *Woomph!* Her breasts crushed against a massive torso, spread across the carpet. A warm breath exhaled in her ear. A low voice grunted a dark oath.

Lionel?

Oh no.

Oh yes.

She struggled briefly to upright herself, but his strong arm clamped her to his solid chest. A free hand roamed her body, patting her waist, her ribs, her side. Then it bumped into her breast, surrounded it, and expertly began to test its volume and shape.

She went completely still.

"Sophie? Bloody hell." His hand covered the fullness of her

long-neglected breast, and his fingers tweaked her nipple. "I thought you were my sons—"

She wasn't his sons. Her nipple peaked, and a spike of pleasure shot into her belly.

"What are you doing here?" they began together.

"You first," he rasped.

"No, you," she choked out. "You're the one on the floor."

"I'm guarding the twins' bloody door," he said in a hoarse tone she'd never heard from him. "But they sleep like logs." He shifted, his hipbone under hers, his hands moving from her breasts to support her waist. "What the devil are you sneaking about for?"

"I'm not sneaking. I'm checking on Simon," she said, awareness of her position and predicament growing.

Awareness of him growing. In her effort to get up, she'd splayed her legs over his hips. Interesting. The insides of her thighs rested on the outsides of his with nothing between them but her night rail and his breeches.

"Rather late for you to be about," Lionel observed as if in casual conversation, but he held her fast against his muscled chest and masculine heat.

"It's not too late for you," she countered reasonably. She didn't feel reasonable. She could hardly breathe. Hardly think. He had to feel the wild hammering of her heart against his chest.

He held her still, and still he grew beneath her, his erection at the parting of her legs as large as any in her bawdy books, poking at her *charms*, her *private place*, her *mound*, her *wem*. Thrills of heat coiled into her belly, deeper than her dreams, sharper than her secret nighttime explorations when she lay abed alone with nothing but the insubstantial stories on a page to suggest that men and women could hold each other in delight and desire.

"Lionel?" she whispered in the silence, filling with hope and fear. There was only the sound of their rhythmic breathing, louder than the ocean's roar. That and the spread of all his heat.

"We have to stop, love," he bit off as if in pain.

"I don't want us to stop," she said.

He groaned, but flattened a large hand on her back and cupped her buttocks with the other, adjusting her against his shaft. She shivered to feel its thick hard shape and pulsing passion, and flushed hot atop his burning member.

Twenty years she'd lived and never been touched like this. She'd felt the hand of a friend, the cheek of a child, the arms of a grieving neighbor. Her father's shoulder when she trimmed his hair. Her life had been so full, and yet she had missed so much.

Hot tears burned her eyes.

She would not let this opportunity pass.

She moved her yearning mound against his heated shaft. His *pillar, column, pego, rod, John Thomas*. Those bawdy books had taught her many words for a man's instrument of pleasure. She'd known no man in the fullness of coition, not even Lionel. But when she'd read those bawdy books, she'd seen lovers in her mind's eye: The lovers of her imagination had all been him, all the male members had been his.

And he was here, for her, at last.

And his shaft burned to possess her, and she could feel his power and her own womb answer to his claim.

With a low fierce growl, he ground his erection upward into her belly. Deep inside she shook with the shock of his desire. His seeking hands found the belt of her nightgown, untied it, and reached in to part its heavy woolen weight aside.

"Tell me to stop, damn it," he whispered harshly at her ear, a curse, a plea, an order. But every puff of his hot breath spiked another thrill of pleasure down her neck.

"Don't stop," she breathed. "Please heaven, don't stop."

With a moan of surrender, he rucked up her night rail with rough hands, baring the skin of her legs and her bottom to the cool night air. Safe in the enveloping darkness of the hall, she gasped at nakedness, at novelty. Coarse linen breeches and cold metal buttons pressed the soft skin of her inner thighs.

But she wanted to feel him. *Him.* Her fingers fumbled with the buttons on either side of his breeches' fall, fumbled but unfastened them one by one, his harsh breathing thrilling at her ear. Then she reached inside to free him, feeling hard muscles under soft skin, his belly, his shaft. Satin over iron, jutting, seeking her hand. She wrapped her fingers round his heat, tears of wonder brimming after all these years. Lionel was fully a man now, with a man's knowledge, a man's urges, a man's hunger.

She understood this without reading it in a book.

She understood it with her heart.

Lionel the rake, father, earl, lover, knew what he wanted from a woman and knew how to take it, knew the needs of women's bodies. His rough hands sought her curves, her limbs, her muscles, possessing her with nothing of the tender questing of the dreamy lad she had given almost everything to. Her womb dipped with yearning. The rake he'd become knew how to pleasure women. He could pleasure her. He could rid her of her burdensome virginity.

He could set her free.

She arched her back and pressed her belly to his, joining her ribs to his, propping on her elbows to lift her breasts slightly away from his chest. His hand on her back snugged her down to him, and her breasts crushed against his chest as it rose and fell with quicker breaths.

He released her arms, and she dug her fingers through his hair. In the dark it had no color, but it capped his skull with short, dense, Byronic curls, rough to touch, untamed, wild, longer than when he'd first come down from London, more like the dreamy lad's. The other hand she wrapped around the thickness of his nape. Its steely cords went taut as he lifted his head toward her.

"This is your last chance," he rasped.

"Last chance for what?" she asked, barely thinking, she was

163

so enthralled with skin and breath and mouth and hair.

"To stop me."

"Don't want to stop you," she murmured, parting her lips and lowering her head, awkwardly seeking him in the blackness. It hid them from others but not from each other. His mouth was soft and silken, but he claimed her with a fierce desire that melted her, her gut, her bones, and inside, in between her legs. She ached there, craving more. His teeth clanged against hers, announcing his siege, insisting on her surrender, and she felt the pressure of his tongue, and then he pulled away, a hairsbreadth of air between them.

"Open your mouth then, Sophie, open now."

He sounded urgent, savage, as he never had that summer or lately at the kissing gate, and she opened to admit him, shocked and thrilled by his fierce feral change. He thrust his tongue into her mouth, a groan of satisfaction humming in his throat, and suddenly she felt all sensation everywhere, the wet, hot slide of his tongue against hers, the hum vibrating into his chest against her aching breasts, and heat spreading from his fiery shaft to the very depth of her womb.

Her legs contracted around him, and a whimper of surprise deepened into strange animal groans, such as she had never uttered. Wave upon wave of shimmering light coursed through her, collected between her legs, and exploded in hot, sharp spikes like lightning flashing in the sky. Even the darkness behind her eyes flared into colors, and she was panting, gasping with the effort and the joy. Then it broke, and her body, still sprawled around him, went slack and settled onto his taut form.

"Dear God, Sophie love, you're so randy," he was whispering in her ear, his hot moist breath sending prickles of desire down her neck and spreading across her shoulders. "Wrap your hand around me, love," he panted. She did, surprised to feel his shaft growing harder and larger even as she held him close, *loved him*, hunched with the aftershocks of her own pleasure. He muttered something unspeakably vulgar that he wanted to do to her, and thrust against her hand, his body rocking her, shaking her even as he spasmed beneath her.

Outside her. His hot, sticky *liquor, juice, seed* spilled over her hand and spread onto the poor thin fabric of her night rail.

He had taken his pleasure outside.

She swallowed against a sob of disappointment.

He must think he'd spared her, but the end was all the same. She was still a virgin. Blast and damn.

Then she heard their agitated breathing, man and woman, not quite joined, partial ecstasy shared, spent, gradually calming.

"Good God, Sophie," he said at last, his voice raspy with hot sex and regret. "Can you forgive me? I can be less the animal but not, it seems, with you."

"If you were an animal," she whispered, "I loved every minute of it. Was I an animal too?"

He gave a harsh, rueful laugh. "God, yes, and you were magnificent. Unwise, but magnificent."

He did not push her away. In her inexperience, she thought her books covered everything. Yet their heated, bawdy, vulgar prose barely scratched the surface of the shimmering, grasping, spiritual, animal, ridiculous, transcendent act she had just shared with Lionel.

He tucked her shoulder under his arm and pressed her cheek to his chest. "Never mind. Lie with me."

Her conscience surfaced long enough for her to murmur, "I should check on Simon."

An ironic laugh rumbled through Lionel's torso. "If he needs us, we will hear him. Lie here, love, shh."

Love, over and over, he'd called her love. Her heart squeezed the sweetness of it, the joy of it; then she mused miserably: *This must be how it is with rakes, all women are their loves.* So be it. She could love a rake, if loving him, if *he,* would free her from the shackles of virginity and teach her to know pleasure.

Exhausted, she drifted to the rhythm of his breathing and the sound of his bounding pulse. Drowsy, deepening into slumber, and then he was tenderly kissing her awake, gently pulling her to her knees, standing her to wakefulness. He eased her dressing gown back onto her shoulders, found its sash and tied it, backward from her usual way.

What a charming touch. The moon poked out from clouds as he adjusted his own clothing, the consideration he had shown her vanishing in angry, jerky movements. Still she watched, reveling in her intimate new knowledge of the comfort of his broad chest and the power of his manhood. The silvery light glinted off his tawny hair and thick straight brows. But his iron-gray eyes turned bleak and somber.

"Damn me for a rogue, Sophie," he said, his voice harsh with regret. "I promised not to harm you."

He was pushing her away again. Again! She would not let him. "I am not harmed, my lord."

"Not harmed!" He swore softly.

She lifted her chin. "I thought that was glorious."

"That's not what you're supposed to think." He grasped her upper arms as if to convince her. "I'm the rake. And a bounder for corrupting one like you."

The languid, vulnerable aftermath of love had enveloped her like a friendly fog. It evaporated, leaving only anger about the one part of her life still incomplete. "*One like me?* Do you think I don't know that men and women make love to one another? Do you suppose I'm pleased that I missed out on that? And how do you propose that I manage my attraction to you while I'm living under your roof? Go deaf and dumb and numb?"

He shook his head sadly. "You're better than I am, Sophie. I'm new at reform."

"I didn't ask you to reform." He had knotted her gown wrong. She angrily untied it and jerked it into her usual knot, pleased to note he was not yet reformed enough to ignore her, dressing or undressing.